HOUSE OF SAGE AND SALT

CHRIS COOPER

DREADFUL
MEDIA

House of Sage and Salt

Published by Dreadful Media

Enjoy the book? Please consider leaving a review at goodreads.com or amazon.com. Every review helps. To receive news of new publications, events, and exclusive offers, please sign up for the Dreadful Media Newsletter on our website. WWW.DREADFULMEDIA.COM

SPECIAL THANKS

Olivia Arscott
Dave Cutler
Aimee Futcher
Aunt Kim
Juliana T. Johnson
Jacob & Taylor Mathers
Rockelle & Tanner Reynolds
Carlos Arturo Soto
Jenni D Strand

PROLOGUE

Emma ran through the foyer as the house creaked and groaned around her. The floorboards shook beneath her feet as she approached the front door. She gripped the knob and twisted frantically, but the door refused to budge, and her hand tingled as if the house had been electrified. The pulleys squealed to life as the single-pane windows in the dining room slid closed, shedding flakes of chipped paint as they ground against their aged wooden frames. The curtain tassels slithered loose from their knots, and the heavy drapes fell slack and slunk along the floor, blocking the moon's glow and trapping her inside a house that had now become her decrepit tomb.

I'm going to die here.

CHAPTER ONE

Two Weeks Earlier

The Aurora was burning oil again. A few wisps of smoke gradually swirled into a hazy trail that followed Emma's car down the highway and filled the cab with a noxious odor. An old man in a red pickup honked and pointed at the tail end of her car as if she hadn't noticed the wall of black following her. As he gestured for her to roll down her window, she couldn't think of a way to tell him she'd taped it shut from the inside months before to keep the rain out.

She pulled off the road and into the nearest gas station as the smell burned her nostrils. She'd kept an extra quart of oil in the trunk for just such an occasion but had used the last of it a few days back. Instead of buying more oil, she'd spent her last few bucks on a frozen pizza and a cheap bottle of cabernet. Her fortunes had shifted within the last twenty-four hours, though. Her hand traced the fresh stack of twenties tucked into her jean pocket. The extra dough improved her chances for not arriving in Rudder by foot or on fire.

Emma pulled her long brown hair back into a ponytail and popped the hood. She looked down at the tangle of hot tubes and pipes as if she'd be able to decipher what any of them did if she stared long enough.

"Need some help, miss?" The man from the red pickup adjusted his ball cap as he stepped toward her.

Emma sighed. "The thing's been burning oil for a few weeks now, and I have no idea what's wrong with it. Haven't had the chance to take it in to get it looked at."

The last line was a lie. Emma knew there was no point in having it looked at if she couldn't afford to fix it.

"Mind if I have a look?"

Emma stepped aside. "Have at it."

The man took off his cap and stuck the bill into his back pocket as he leaned over the hood. After a few pokes and prods, he emerged with a grin.

"What is it?" She saw dollar signs flashing in her mind's eye, and a knot formed in her stomach.

"An easy fix, most likely. Next time you pass an auto shop, tell 'em you need a PCV valve. It'll cost you three bucks."

She could have hugged the man if hugging had been her thing. "Thank you." Her voice carried a slight quiver.

"No problem, miss. You take care of yourself, now. And get that fixed." He ran his hand through his thinning hair and slid his cap back on.

Emma bought a quart of oil and fed most of it to the hungry engine before shutting the hood and climbing back into the driver's seat. She ran her hands along the steering wheel. "Looks like you'll live to see another day."

The Aurora had been her closest brush with luxury in recent memory, but it was a twenty-five-year-old luxury that came with balding tires and leaky valves. Still, the car got her from her apartment to her part-time retail job and back without too much protest. The cross-country road trip, on the other hand, was another story, and her stomach lurched with every strange engine groan and belt squeak. If the job panned out, she'd find a used car that didn't feel as if it was perpetually on the verge of spontaneously combusting.

Emma grabbed her phone from the passenger seat and adjusted her black horn-rimmed glasses as she reread the cryptic text conversation from earlier that week.

Adam: *Want to make an extra five grand this month?*
Emma: *Bullshit! Has your phone been hacked?*
Adam: *Nope, just thought you could use the extra $$$.*
Emma: *Something legal?*

Adam: *As legal as it gets. AND you'll have a free creepy house to stay in.*

The text had come from her brother, Adam, after several months of radio silence. She might have blown off his offer if he hadn't repaid the five hundred bucks he'd borrowed to "get myself out of trouble" as a goodwill gesture. Even if the job fell through, as it probably would, she'd still have enough gas money to get home. Thinking of the recent rift between her and Adam made her chest tighten. They'd always been close, and she held out hope that the invite to this impromptu Tennessee adventure was an olive branch.

She switched to her GPS app and resumed the route to her destination as the sun set over the horizon. The drive from upstate New York had taken the better part of two days, including a terrifying night in a run-down rest-stop parking lot. Her cellphone bars dwindled until she lost high-speed service altogether. *Almost there,* she thought as she spotted her exit up ahead.

After pulling off at the exit, Emma drove several miles down the two-lane road until her GPS signaled for her to turn onto an old dirt path that led to a portal of over-hanging trees framing an entrance to the woods. She double-checked the address to ensure that she was headed in the right direction.

She wondered what harebrained scheme her brother

had gotten himself into. His life had been peppered with bad luck and poor choices, and any job that paid ten grand had to be more complicated than it seemed. No, she was certain he'd gotten himself wrapped up in a perverted sex cult or an underground murder society where they'd both be auctioned off to the highest bidder.

"Take a breath, Emma," she said aloud, making eye contact with herself in the rearview mirror. "Rent, new tires, and a laptop that doesn't shut down if you jiggle the power cable." Her eyes darted to the useless hunk of plastic in the back seat. "Plus, if it's a sex cult, it's been a while since you've had any action."

Limbs scraped the roof of her car like hundreds of tiny clawing creatures as she pulled through the tree line. Trunks clung tightly to the narrow road in places, and she watched her side mirror carefully to avoid clipping it on the remnants of rock wall that had been cleared for the shoddy road.

Emma rolled the passenger window down as sounds of flowing water and shifting trees filtered in with a cool autumn breeze. She stopped the car to listen, and Jeff Buckley blared from her car stereo and echoed through the forest before she cut the engine altogether. Wind swept through the trees, sending a flurry of orange and yellow leaves cascading to the forest floor, and the natural white noise blocked any sounds of distant traffic. The air was crisp but not as cold as it likely would be within the coming days. Water trickled through a brook below.

She breathed deeply. A few weeks in the woods couldn't be that bad. She'd have a creepy house to provide inspiration for her book and maybe even a nice stack of cash when she went back to New York.

Her heart fluttered every time she thought of the book. *The book* was a sprawling gothic tale that had been a work in progress for three months now, and although she had little more to show for it than a title page, she had tons of ideas. But at least the title page was perfect, except for the fact she had yet to settle on a title. She fidgeted with the steering wheel and took another deep breath. She might have had a freshly minted English degree in hand, but life since graduation hadn't been the happily ever after she'd hoped for. She'd envisioned headlines about a literary wunderkind, straight out of college and equipped to conquer the world, but life had other plans. Her short stories had garnered zero attention, and she hoped a book would finally set her dreams in motion.

A rustling pulled Emma from her existential crisis, and she searched the tree line for the source of the sound— probably just squirrels chasing each other up the side of an oak. Stress would likely kill her before any hatchet-wielding madman could.

The Aurora sputtered to life and spat out another cloud of black smoke. As she floored the gas pedal up the final bend, she turned her head just in time to see a set of wrought-iron gates rise out of the darkness and slammed her brakes to avoid barreling into them. The Aurora's headlights shone through the slats, and she could just make out the black silhouette of the mammoth structure in the clearing on the other side.

Welcome to Hill House. Hope I'm not the crazy one. She reached for her phone and tapped Adam's face on her contact list. *Straight to voicemail. What an ass.* "Home sweet home, I guess."

The iron spindles of the gate formed a decorative floral filigree that ran the length of the fence. The gate itself was at least twice her height and sandwiched between two imposing stone pillars. Her eyes traced the flowers to the gate's crest, an all-seeing eye housing a keyhole in its pupil. *You're definitely going in the book.*

Emma wrapped her hands around one of the metal spindles and pushed. The gate squealed open, and she stepped onto the gravel path on the other side. The house had no exterior lighting and was nothing more than a massive black outline speckled with lit windows that seemed to float in space.

She pulled the other side of the gate open until she had enough clearance for the car. The beams from her headlights bounced off her brother's Honda. She pulled her car next to Adam's and grabbed her duffel bag and laptop. The front door sat open, and flickering firelight floated out into the entryway, providing just enough glow to light her path to the front door. As she approached, her ear caught the tinny music drifting through the entryway. The singer's voice warped and wavered and sounded as if it came from a record someone had left in the sun for too long.

Emma ran her fingers along the cool stone of the doorway as she crossed the threshold, and the loose hardwood planks in the foyer creaked underfoot. "Hello." The foyer had dumped her into a cavernous dining room, and her voice echoed off its wainscoted walls.

A heavy oak table sat in the center of the room with an ornate chandelier hanging above it. The firelight from the neighboring room cast an eerie glow while making it impossible to see the corners of the dining space so that it looked endless. The air was cool and damp like that of the old Scottish castles she'd visited for one of her writing classes.

"Hello." Emma followed the music to the living room, her heart fluttering with a mix of macabre curiosity and anticipatory terror. She crossed to an antique record player and lifted the needle to stop the strange music. As she turned and approached the fire, seeking its protective warmth, she noticed a form splayed on the ground in front of the dusty sofa. Her brother lay lifeless, and the fire caught a red halo puddled around his head and an iron fire poker lying next to him.

"Adam." Her voice came out in a wavering whisper.

She knelt and examined the unnaturally red substance next to him. After a moment of hesitation, she ran two fingers through the sticky splotch of blood on his forehead and brought them to her lips. "Corn syrup? What are you, five? You'll have to do better than that."

His eyes shot open. "Can't blame a guy for trying," he said with a hint of disappointment. Adam reached out a bloody hand, and Emma helped him to his feet.

"You should've tried something new. You pulled that trick on Mom and Dad when you pretended to fall down the steps, remember?"

"Do I remember? I was grounded for three weeks." He leaned in and wrapped his arms around her. "Good to see you, Em."

She rested her head on his shoulder, and for a moment, it felt as if the recent tension between them had evaporated. "Good to see you too. Please tell me you didn't bring me all the way out here for a bad joke."

"You think I'd have given you five hundred bucks? No offense, but scaring you isn't worth the kind of dough. Come with me. Gotta grab a rag from the kitchen."

"You mean, the five hundred you borrowed from me?" she shot back.

Adam turned toward her. "Still bitter, I see. Guess I should be bitter about you calling me a perceptual failure, then."

Emma clenched her fist. "*Perpetual* failure, and facts aren't always friendly facts."

Adam spun around, closed his eyes, and took a deep breath. "Well, that's in the past. No point being mad about things we can't change."

Easy for him to say. "But seriously. The job is real, right? You didn't bring me all the way out here for a gag, did you?"

"Oh, the job *is* real, and it's much more than a job. We have an amazing opportunity!" He gestured around the room. "Look at this place!"

Although the light was dim, Emma could see layers upon layers of dust. Stacks of old newspapers sat in the corners, and the place looked as if it hadn't been cleaned in years.

"Opportunity—right." She followed him to the kitchen. "So what exactly are we doing here?"

"Getting paid." He pulled a wet rag from the kitchen sink and brought it back to the living room.

"I'm serious. Why are we here?"

He laughed. "Happy to see you too. Look, it's too late to do anything tonight, so why don't we just enjoy each other's company, and I'll fill you in in the morning?" He wiped the fake blood from his hair then scrubbed the patch on the floor.

"Cut the bullshit. Tell me why you brought me out here."

"You're no fun."

Emma put her hand on her hip.

"Fine. A scavenger hunt," he replied.

"Someone's paying you to do a scavenger hunt?"

"We're in a big old house full of stuff the new owner doesn't want, except for one particular item."

"Which is...?" she asked.

"An antique book of some sort."

"The owner's going to pay us thousands of dollars to find a book?"

"I guess it's worth way more than a few thousand bucks." Adam scrubbed the remainder of the sticky red goop from the floor then returned to the kitchen to clean the rag. "So, how have you been, sis? It's been ages."

Her grip tightened on the fire poker. "You're telling me. You've been ignoring my texts. Do you know what it's been like to deal with Mom and Dad while you've been AWOL for a year? Mom's convinced you're dead."

"Would you relax? If we're going to spend the next few weeks together, we shouldn't start it off with a fight. I'll deal with Mom and Dad. Think of this as a big vacation. You can work on your book! Speaking of, how's that going?" He grinned.

Emma dug the heels of her sneakers into the floor. "Great."

"See? Soon, you'll be a famous author."

Or a wannabe hack, she thought.

"Tell you what. Why don't I take you to your bedroom, you can get washed up, and we'll hang out. Since they don't deliver pizza this far out, I stopped by the store on the way in. I'll make dinner."

Adam led her back through the foyer to the staircase. Faded crimson carpet covered the steps, lined with zigzag shapes that were barely visible amidst the dirt and dander. Dust motes floated around Emma's ankles as she climbed the steps.

"So, when is the new owner moving in?" she asked.

"Dunno. The old lady who lived here before must have croaked a few weeks ago. And not a moment too soon. I was running low on funds."

Emma punched him on the back of the shoulder. "Have some tact, would you, you ape?"

Adam snorted. "What? She can't hear me."

Flames from the lit wall sconces cast flickering shadows on the dingy wallpaper. Emma ran her finger along a bookshelf as they passed and immediately regretted it as a thick coating of dust clumped on her fingertip. "Not much of a housekeeper, was she?"

"I'm guessing she didn't have many guests," he replied. "I figured I'd set you up in her bedroom—"

"No way!" Emma pulled back.

"Just kidding. The house has, like, five. The one down the hall's nice."

Emma couldn't see his face but knew he was smirking. "Reassuring."

"Just a word of warning: this place must use a well, because all the water reeks. It should still be safe to drink, but I'll pick up some bottled water tomorrow just in case."

"Fantastic." Emma opened the bedroom door. Her eyes met the gaze of a gray ghost, and she jumped backward into the hallway.

Adam let out a cackle. "Figured you'd like that."

Emma took another look inside. A hodgepodge of black-and-white portraits lined the bedroom walls. The glossed-over gazes of long-dead strangers cut through her. "And why would you think this is a good room to put me in?"

He snickered. "You like all this creepy stuff, right? Think of it as research. Get to know your characters."

Emma scowled.

"All right, I admit I collected a few of these from the other bedrooms. I just thought you'd want some company."

She reached into her duffel bag and pulled her phone cord from an end pocket. "My phone's about to die. Help me find a plug, would you?" She looked at the burning oil lamp on the dresser and started to piece things together—the hand-cranked record player, the candles, the oil lamps. "Please tell me this place has electricity."

Adam ran his hand along the wall next to the dresser,

and with a loud snap of an old-fashioned button switch, the chandelier lit up and cast a dingy glow over the room. His toothy grin was a putrid yellow under the dim overhead light.

Emma found an outlet underneath the small writing desk and plugged in her phone adapter. She yawned loudly and checked the time on her phone. "I'm pretty wiped from driving, actually. Do you care if we catch up tomorrow?"

"Sounds good to me. Bathroom is across the hall, and I'll be downstairs if you need me," he said in singsong as he turned toward the hallway.

"Hey," she called after him.

"Yeah?"

"I am glad to see you."

"Glad to see you, too, Em. Now, get some sleep. We've got work to do in the morning. And enjoy the company!" His voice trailed off down the hall.

Emma threw her duffel bag on the floor and laid her laptop on the writing desk. As she approached the bed, she locked eyes with a portrait. The woman, perhaps a few years older than her, stared back. Her hair was pulled into a tight bun, and the stiff collar of her dress clung tightly to her neck. The lower lids of her tired eyes sagged and were underlined by deep bags that the black-and-white photo couldn't hide. Emma pulled her hair down from her ponytail and let it drape over her shoulders as her eyes traced the woman's silhouette. She pulled the frame from the wall and flipped it over. *Rosalie* was etched in pencil with *1955* written below it.

I'm tired, too, Rosalie. She hung the photo once more and fell backward in dramatic fashion onto the old mattress. A plume of dust consumed her. *He could have at least changed the damn sheets.*

CHAPTER TWO

A loud bang pulled Emma from a dream. She lay facedown on a lace pillow with a long tangle of brown hair pressed into the side of her face. She wiped the corners of her mouth and rolled over, for a moment not sure where she was. A sliver of sunlight danced on the opposite wall as it broke through the shifting gap in the heavy curtains.

Emma pulled back the spare sheets she'd found in the hall closet the night prior. The bed was comfortable once she'd removed the dusty linens, probably taking a hundred years of dead skin cells with them. She'd also pulled the creepy family portraits down and stacked them facing the wall—all but the one of Rosalie, which she left in place for a reason she couldn't quite explain.

Her phone had charged but was useless without a signal. The entire room was a dead zone. She slipped on a pair of sweatpants and stepped into the hall. Although the bedroom radiator had kept her room warm and cozy, a cold draft blew through the hallway. Adam stood at the top of the steps.

"Why are you making so much noise?" she asked.

Another clang echoed up the staircase.

"It's not me," he whispered.

The hairs on the back of Emma's neck stood on end. "Are you screwing with me again?" She balled her hands into fists.

Adam shook his head. "How would I mess with you from up here?"

Emma's eyes darted to the staircase.

Adam tiptoed toward the edge of the steps. "Stay here," he mouthed.

If this turned out to be another joke, Emma resolved to push him down the steps the next time she had a chance.

He reached for the door of the hallway closet, slipped inside, and emerged holding an old corn broom with a long wooden handle. He cocked his arm back and held the broom like a baseball bat as he descended. If he was joking, he was fully committed to the charade but could have chosen a better weapon.

Emma watched until he disappeared around the corner into the foyer, the floorboards still creaking as he continued out of sight. She listened intently for any other sounds over her short panicked breaths.

"All clear!" he shouted.

Emma hurried down the stairs and joined him in the kitchen.

He stared at two cast-iron pans that had fallen from the ceiling rack. "The hooks must have come loose."

"What are the odds of that? That thing has probably been hanging for decades."

He shrugged. "Maybe Casper was trying to make us breakfast." He knelt to pick up the cookware.

"He's doing a terrible job. What do we have for breakfast, anyway?" She turned toward the powder-blue refrigerator and pulled the handle.

"No, don't!" Adam reached for her, but she'd already broken the seal.

The smell of putrid rotting meat burned her nostrils, and she gagged as she pulled her head away.

Adam covered his nose with his sweater sleeve. "Sorry, should have warned you."

Emma retched again as she stepped over to the sink and turned the water on. "It smells like hot garbage," she said between gags. She splashed her face then recoiled.

"Don't forget the well water," he added.

"I can't win!" She marched through the back door and into the yard, sucking in the fresh morning air.

Adam chased after her. "I'm sorry. I meant to tell you the fridge's compressor must have died sometime within the last fifty years. I couldn't stand the smell long enough to clean it out. All our food's in a cooler."

"At least I'm awake now." She blinked hard and tried to squelch the burn in her eyes.

"We're going to need to let that air out for a minute." Adam pulled a chair from a patio table and gestured for Emma to sit.

"I thought you said the lady died a few weeks ago."

He sat next to her. "I may have misspoken. They found her body a few weeks ago, but apparently, it had been there for a while."

"So she died alone? What happened to her?"

"Natural causes. The deliveryman found her when he came with the groceries. I guess she'd never taken the last order inside, and he thought something was up, so he came in to check on her. She was a hermit, apparently."

Emma sat back in her chair. "How awful that must have been. What was her name?"

"Dunno. Why?"

Emma looked out into the backyard. "I think it might be Rosalie. The name was written on the back of one of the portraits in the bedroom. The others would have been too old, but this one was dated 1955."

"Your guess is as good as mine," he replied.

"And the new owner is a relative?"

"I didn't ask and don't care, to be honest. All I know is

he'll pay us ten grand if we find his book by the end of the month." He mouthed "ten grand" again for emphasis.

Emma scowled. "I thought about that last night, and it still doesn't make sense. A book in this house is so valuable someone will pay ten grand just to get it back, but that person is too busy to come and get it himself?"

"Rich people can't be bothered, I guess." Adam grinned widely.

"And why the hell would they trust *you* to get it if it's so valuable?"

Adam crossed his arms as his smile faded. "You're not showing a lot of gratitude to the person who just cut you in for fifty percent of a ten-thousand-dollar deal. All we have to do is find a stupid book."

"Because the deal is asinine. Why wouldn't he just come and get it himself, and who is this person? How do you know you're not being scammed?"

Adam averted his eyes.

"How did you even find out about this?"

Silence.

"Tell me, or I'm getting back into my car and driving away."

"Brandon," Adam murmured.

"Brandon? That asshole nearly got you thrown into jail!"

Adam waved his hand dismissively. "That was a long time ago. Look, Brandon's really got his shit together. He weaseled himself into a job tracking down items for antique dealers, and—"

"By 'tracking down,' you mean *stealing*."

"No, it's legit. He travels all over the world to do this stuff now, and he makes bank doing it. Someone approached him about this place and the book, and he was too busy to take the job, so he threw it my way. He knew I needed the extra cash. I thought it would be good for us, you know, to spend a little time together now that you're out of school and before you go getting all famous from your novel."

Emma snorted.

Adam cocked his head. "I'm serious. I know I haven't always made the best decisions, but I checked this out. Brandon passed my name to the guy who wants the book, and we met. He gave me the keys and a deposit and showed me the deed to prove he wasn't full of shit. He owns this place. I've done my research, Em. I'm not gonna let you down this time. I owe you. I know you couldn't afford to help me out, but you did it anyway. And I thought it might actually be nice to spend some time together—to get things back to normal."

Emma bit her lower lip. "That may be, but it still doesn't explain why he doesn't come here himself."

"You've only seen a piece of this place—it's huge. The guy's probably just a busy dude and doesn't have the time to go around searching for rare books. You'll see once I show you the library. And I met him upstate. I guess he just doesn't have the time to drive all the way down here."

"That is a long drive." She shot him an angry glance. "You were in town, and you didn't bother to come by? You didn't bother to go see Mom and Dad?"

Adam shuffled uncomfortably in his chair then reached over and squeezed Emma's arm. "I'll deal with them later. I promise. This will be good for both of us. And I know you could use the money. I've seen that piece-of-shit car parked out front. So let's not make this more stressful than it has to be. We've got nearly two weeks. We'll take the search room by room, and you can write in between. You could finish your book in two weeks."

Emma rubbed her temples. "I've been working on it for three months, and so far I've written jack squat. So far, I'm a catastrophic failure."

Adam jumped up from his chair. "See! All the more reason to cut yourself some slack. You're too stressed about it. Let the environment inspire you." He gestured wildly. "There's so much cool shit here."

Emma took in a deep breath and exhaled loudly. "You're right. You're right. I always overthink things."

"When have I ever steered you wrong?"

She shot him a look. "You really want to ask that question?"

"Okay, maybe a better question would be, when have I steered you wrong recently?"

Emma hopped up from her chair. "Show me around the place before I change my mind."

Adam clapped his hands together. "That's my girl! We can start the tour right here. Behold the glorious backyard garden."

A tall stone wall bordered the backyard, topped with wrought-iron spikes. The left corner of the garden had succumbed to weeds, while an old shed teetered on the brink of collapse on the right. A patchwork of powdery white plants covered the rest of the garden, overgrown and untamed by human intervention. She and Adam strolled down the gravel path, although most of it had been taken over by the mysterious white plant.

Emma knelt and pulled a leaf free then rubbed it in between her thumb and index finger. "It's fuzzy, like Lamb's Ear." She held the leaves up to her nose. "Oh, definitely sage."

"Sage? Isn't that, like, a spice?"

She took another whiff to clear the hint of rotting food still clinging to the inside of her nostrils. "An herb, I think. What a weird thing to grow out here. You'd think she'd have some tomato plants at least, especially if she was such a shut-in."

"Yeah, because we're clearly dealing with a woman playing with a full deck. It's not normal to live out in the wilderness all alone."

"Thoreau did it." Emma stepped through the tangle of

plants to the back shed and pulled on the rotted wooden door. "Think we'll find her husband in here?"

Rusted garden tools leaned against the far wall, and bundled plants hung from the rafters in neat rows.

"Did we just find the old lady's pot stash?" he asked, his eyes aglow with hope.

"More sage. I have a friend who burns it. You hang it up to dry like this then bundle it up and burn it."

"Kind of overkill, don't you think?"

Emma shrugged. "Maybe she just likes the smell."

She turned toward the back of the house. She hadn't seen the exterior in the daylight. What she'd thought was two stories turned out to be a three-story stone structure. Moss covered the first-floor stonework, while wood shakes tiled the second and third. A stone chimney stretched to the sky, even with the crest of the third-floor roof. That floor appeared to be no larger than a single room. Emma had to remind herself that she was in Tennessee and not some foreign country.

"You notice the gargoyles?" Adam asked.

A perimeter of gargoyles came into focus as she squinted up at the roof. She counted three on the back of the house, two mounted atop the rotundas on either side, and a third perched on a stone pediment in the center, each staring down upon the backyard and surrounding area.

"When do you think they built this place? It's got to be

at least a hundred years old, right? But who puts gargoyles on their house?"

Adam shrugged.

"I want to see the front." She took the gravel path around the side of the house, with Adam in tow. They passed a small greenhouse that was tucked against the stone foundation and speckled with shattered clay pots and shards of glass.

She ran her hands along the stone walls, her fingers catching on holes and cracked stones as she passed. Some shakes above her hung loose against the side of the house, pulling free where water had penetrated the failing paint and caused the wood to rot. She reached up and pulled one of the wooden scales, and it crumbled in her hands. "This place is in rough shape."

A dead rosebush obscured the walkway and scratched them as they squeezed through to the front yard. Two more rotundas were tacked onto either side of the front of the house. A balcony poked out of the third-floor roof, and a curved window protruded from the attached room. The roof itself sagged in the middle, and much like Rosalie, the house appeared to need a long nap.

Emma rubbed her chin. "This building doesn't make any sense. It's like the designer took a bunch of different styles and just squashed them all together." She looked across the yard at the metal gate and the imposing woods beyond. "What a strange place to build a house like this. How'd they even get all the materials out here?"

"One stone at a time?"

"And probably slaves," Emma added.

"There's a story hook for you. Creepy house in the woods, haunted by those who died building it." He looked toward the house with a solemn expression. "They found freedom only in death, and now they're back for revenge —*House of a Thousand Chains*."

Emma laughed. "Maybe you should write a book. You might have better luck."

"Don't be so hard on yourself. Come on, let me show you the library. If you think the outside's interesting..."

Emma had started to piece bits of the narrative together as they approached the front steps. The house hadn't been built by slaves, she decided. It was a living, breathing thing that fed off those who inhabited it. The house sustained itself with their energy. And Emma had found the name of the story's main character—Rosalie.

Adam held the front door open for Emma. "You know those turrets? The living room runs into one, the dining room into another, and the kitchen into the third." They walked toward the back of the house. "But the fourth... that houses the library."

They came to a door on the other side of the kitchen, just past the back patio.

Adam hit the switch on the wall, and the light came on,

illuminating the intricately carved door in front of them. Like the gate, it held an eye in the center, etched deep into the wood with chevrons radiating out of it like jagged beams of light. "Look at this thing." He lifted the iron door ring and twisted, shifting the wooden latch out of the way. "Behold, the library!" With a heave, he pushed the door open into the room on the other side.

The circular room expanded upward toward a conical roof. Curved bookshelves, separated by ringed metal walkways, lined the walls and extended to the ceiling. A sliding ladder hung from each shelf, and a spiral staircase shot up from the ground floor through each metal platform.

Light beamed down from the roof skylight, and Adam crossed through its rays and sat at a reading desk perched in the center of the epic library. "What do you think?"

Emma felt as if she'd have to push her mouth closed. The room reminded her of a miniature version of the library at Trinity College in Dublin, or at least the pictures she'd seen of it. "I think our book search starts here. Where's the card catalogue?" She grinned.

"I wish we could read them. I checked a few books, and most of them are in Latin or other squiggly languages I don't recognize." He rested his feet on the desk's leather pad.

"So, what kind of book are we looking for? The lady's diary?"

"A book with a face."

"A face?" She scowled.

"The guy said we'd know it when we saw it. The cover's made of black leather with a face on the front."

Emma looked up at the swirl of books surrounding her, and her stomach grumbled. "Maybe we should make breakfast first. I'd kill for a cup of coffee."

"Go check the cooler," he replied.

They left the library and made their way back through the house. As Emma entered the kitchen, she walked into a wall of stink. Instead of dissipating, the smell from the fridge seemed to cling to the surfaces of the room like nicotine. She gagged as she crossed to the blue cooler perched in the corner.

"No way we're cooking in here," Adam said from the doorway. "The smell's not exactly good for the appetite. There's a town down the road. Maybe we should head up that way and try to find a place for breakfast."

Emma reached over and cranked the window open above the sink. "We should have opened this earlier. Maybe it'll air out by the time we get back."

"I'll drive," he replied as they stepped into the foyer. "No way I'm riding in that death trap you call a car."

Emma rolled her eyes. "Lead the way, your highness."

CHAPTER THREE

Emma grabbed a book off the pile in the passenger seat of Adam's car. "What's this for?"

Adam snatched it from her and chucked it into the back. "Just dull adult stuff. Throw all that crap in the back."

Emma tossed the stack into the back seat then shoved a pile of fast food bags onto the floorboard to make room. As they pulled through the gate, Emma rolled her window down and let her arm hang slack to catch the cool autumn breeze. Eventually, the winding road dumped them out at the edge of the woods.

"Where's breakfast?" Emma asked.

"Town's another five minutes up the road. And I use the word *town* loosely. *Meth-addled hellhole* might be more accurate."

"How elitist of you."

Emma had heard of towns with one traffic light, but Rudder was the first she'd seen in person. A smattering of abandoned trailers and farmhouses sat on the outskirts, and the blacktop road through the square had large cracks and divots running through it. Emma spotted a general store with a row of boarded-up windows on each side. A two-pump gas station sat opposite.

Adam's eyes traced the broken landscape. "Couldn't see this place well in the dark, but yikes."

Emma feigned disappointment. "I guess my hopes for a Chili's are dashed."

"There's a diner right up ahead, I think."

"Yeah, I see it, right next to that beautiful used-car—er, junkyard."

"I think that's the parking lot." Adam pulled into the lot and parked between the faded paint lines, next to a Frankenstein Oldsmobile with doors in two different colors.

The diner had no name. The front of its backlit sign must have fallen loose, exposing the shattered tube lights underneath. A poster board affixed to the window with tape read, *Diner, Cash Only*.

Adam pointed. "And look, there's a bar next door in case we want to experience the Rudder nightlife."

The bells danced on the glass as Emma opened the door. The place was a typical greasy spoon with scratched linoleum tabletops and cracked vinyl booths. Some black letters on the menu board above the order window were missing, unless *ha burgers* and *milk hakes* were some kind of local specialty.

For a town so dead and desolate, its diner was packed. Emma and Adam found a pair of vacant bar stools. Emma's wobbled and squeaked as she swiveled toward the counter. She eyed the quad burner next to a stack of coffee cups. "Coffee, thank God."

"Best coffee in town," the waitress said, catching her by surprise. "Only coffee in town, really." She smiled wide, her pearly whites framed by ruby-red lipstick as she set two cups on the counter, filling one for Emma. "One for you, too, sweetie?" She tipped the pot in Adam's direction.

"Absolutely," he replied.

Tendrils of black beehive hairdo bounced against her face as she leaned over the counter to pour. Her yellowed name tag read *Agnes* in faded black letters. "Y'all don't look very familiar. Are you from around here?"

Emma cradled the coffee in her hands and singed her mouth with a premature sip. "We're from upstate New York."

Agnes put her hand on her hip. "Ooh, fancy. What brings you down this way?"

Emma gave Adam the side-eye.

"We're spending a few days up in the woods," he replied.

"The woods?" Agnes pointed across the diner. "Out that way?"

Adam nodded.

"You came all the way from New York to go camping out here?" Agnes wasn't an idiot. She turned to address a man waving for her attention at the far end of the bar and held up her index finger.

"Yeah. Maybe you could help us." Adam put his elbows on the counter and leaned in. "We came across this old house, a really odd-looking place out in the woods. Looks like a castle and has a big front gate with an eye on it. Know anything about it?"

Agnes knocked the coffeepot on the edge of the counter, drawing the attention of the counter dwellers next to them. "What are you all doing up there? That's a terrible place to camp. You should go farther south. Fishing's better that way too. There's even a campground the next town over." She pulled her glasses down to the tip of her nose and looked at them over the frames. "You all don't look like roughing-it types."

"So, you do know what I'm talking about, right?" Adam pressed.

Agnes cleared her throat. "Honey, you won't find the locals anywhere near that place. Never been myself and never plan to go. A few kids go up that way now and then and snoop around the outside for a good scare. Most swear it's haunted. Others say it gets under your skin. If you get too close, you feel it in your gut, like someone's watching you." Agnes stared into the distance, then her eyes snapped back to them. "But that's just what I've heard, and people round here tend to make up stories. There's not much else to do in this town but storytelling."

"Know who lives there?" Adam looked like he was reveling in Agnes's discomfort.

"Dunno if anyone lives there anymore. There used to be an old biddy, but she never came to town. Refused. Heard through the grapevine she passed a few weeks ago, but like I said before, no one's going near that place."

"Hey, Agnes!" The man at the far end of the counter held up his empty coffee cup. "Gettin' thirsty over here."

"Coming, babycakes." Agnes turned toward Adam and Emma. "I'll be back for your orders in just a minute."

"You don't know when to stop, do you?" Emma took a cautious sip from her coffee cup. "We don't want people here thinking we're up there snooping around."

"I'm just having a little fun, and what does it matter?" He swiveled toward her. "We've got a legitimate reason to be there, and it's none of their business. Plus, if the town thinks the place is haunted, no one will bother us. And what if the place *is* haunted? That would be fun, right?" He wiggled his fingers in Emma's face, mimicking a ghost. "That's inspiration for you. Speaking of stories, you never told me what the book's about."

Emma stirred her coffee and stared down into swirls.

"It's hard to explain, but I've gotten a few new ideas from the house already. And I think *Rosalie* makes a nice character name. So thanks for hanging up those old pictures."

Adam leaned in and waited for her to continue. "And?"

"And what?" She glanced up at him. "It takes time to come up with a good story. I've been researching the thing for nearly three months now, and I'm trying to add in details from the house."

"What have you been researching? Poltergeists? Ouija boards?"

Emma set her coffee cup on the counter. "You want to know the truth?"

"Always."

"I usually end up reading BuzzFeed articles or watching YouTube. If it's a productive day, I'll solve a good chunk of the *New York Times* crossword puzzle." Emma looked down at her lap as blood rushed to her cheeks.

"You haven't written anything, have you?"

"Not a word of story. Just pages of notes."

"So what's stopping you?" He took a sip from his coffee cup.

"I don't know. Every time I sketch out an idea, I feel like I need to do more research, or it won't work, or it's too much like something I've read."

"You'll get there." He put a hand on her knee and squeezed.

"I hope so. You know, one girl in my graduating class has already sold a few of her short stories, and apparently, she's been picked up by an agent."

"What's her name?"

"Becky."

"Becky—what a bitchy name."

Emma laughed.

"You all ready to order?" Agnes asked from behind the counter.

Adam eyed the menu. "Two eggs, scrambled, hash browns, bacon, and toast." He handed the laminated menu to Agnes.

"What about you, darling?" she asked Emma.

"Just a short stack with sausage links."

Agnes tucked the menus back into the stack on the counter and added the ticket to the order wheel. "It'll be right out."

"I'm serious, though," Adam continued. "If I let my past determine my future, I'd still be selling things that had mysteriously fallen off the backs of trucks."

"Is that why you have all those training books in your car? You didn't think I'd let that go, did you?"

Adam rubbed his forehead. "I've got a friend upstate that's going to get me a job in car insurance. I could end up owning my own business one day. I guess it's still kinda stealing, but at least it's legitimate."

"That's great news!" Emma sat up straighter on her

stool. "Why are you just now telling me about this? Have you told Mom and Dad?"

"I want to make sure it pans out first. Don't want to disappoint them again."

"For what it's worth, I'm proud of you," Emma said.

"Thanks, Em. I figure I'll use the cash we get from this to find a new place, without roommates, and float until the job's finalized. Then you can expect a phone call from me about some fantastic insurance rates."

After breakfast, Adam paid the tab, and they returned to the parking lot. "What do you say we head back and take a stroll through the library?" he asked.

"I'll dust off my Latin," she replied as Adam pulled the car out of the spot and pulled onto the main drag. "What do you think people do around here?"

"Farm maybe? That, or there's probably some big factory or mine nearby."

"Think you could live in a place like this, away from everything?"

"No way in hell," he replied.

"I don't know. I bet I could if I found a little piece of land surrounded by trees. As long as I had an internet connection, I'd be fine."

"Well, once we find this book, we'll ask the guy if the place is for sale." He snickered. "I'm sure he's not eager to move out to the middle of nowhere."

"Only if the place isn't haunted. I'd rather not have roommates."

Clouds tumbled in, coating the blue sky with nebulous gray fluff, as Adam pulled the car through the portal of crooked trees and onto the winding road to the house. "How long do you think it'll take to tackle those bookshelves?" he asked.

"I don't know. A few days maybe?"

As the car pulled through the clearing, Emma noticed the wrought-iron gate. "That's weird. We left the gate open, didn't we?"

Adam climbed out of the car and pushed the gate open to pull the car through. "It is a little loose on the hinges. A storm's rolling in. Maybe the wind blew it shut."

"Could be," she replied.

After he shut the gate behind them, they strolled along the path to the front door. "Shall we get to work?" he asked.

———

CHAPTER FOUR

E mma stood in the center of Rosalie's library as the massive collection of books spiraled around her. By her loose calculations—very loose, considering she'd nearly failed every math class she'd ever taken—the shelves held several thousand books. The soles of her sneakers clanked on the metal stairs as she climbed the spiral staircase to the top, while Adam hesitated on the first step.

"Be careful up there!" Adam shouted from below. "That walkway's probably a hundred years old, and who knows how safe it is."

"It's fine." She waved back at him as she bounced up and down on the top platform. "See? Stable. You just focus on the ground floor, and we'll meet in the middle."

Although life had gifted Adam unearned confidence in most areas, it had forgotten to take away his fear of heights. As a kid, Emma had teetered fearlessly on outlook railings and canyon barricades during the family trip to the Grand Canyon. Meanwhile, Adam had followed at a safe distance like a lost duckling—when he wasn't stealing cheap souvenirs from the gift shops. She found satisfaction in facing a fear her brother couldn't.

Unlike the *Reader's Digests* Emma had found in the upstairs hallway, the books on the library shelves were anything but mass productions. Many were leather bound, some of them thick, some thin, and all slightly different heights and in varying states of decay. She ran her finger along the spine of a tall tome with a cracked leather binding held together by a few twists of thread. When she pulled it loose from the shelf, a layer of sediment came with it, and Emma's resulting sneeze sent another puff of dust into the atmosphere. The leather crinkled and cracked as she opened the cover. The pages inside were yellowed with age and thicker than normal paper. She scratched the bottom edge of the cover page, letting her nail hit the grooves in its surface like a needle skipping across a record. *Linen.* She'd seen books like this in museums, but to hold one in her hand felt wrong, as if she were handling a piece of history that ought to have been locked behind a glass display.

Emma held the book over the railing. "You sure he just wants the one book? I'm no expert, but these must be worth a fortune."

"They're just books."

She pulled another from the shelf and flipped through. "Some of these are handwritten—like, before printing presses—and the work's incredible."

Adam leaned against the edge of the staircase and looked up at her. "How much money are we talking?"

"I don't know. One of my professors told us about a book that sold for millions at auction." Emma could see Adam's gaping mouth from three floors up.

"Think anyone would notice if we took one? Even if we could sell it for ten grand, we'd double our money."

"Are you serious?" She leaned over the railing and stared down at him. "What's all this bullshit about being on the straight and narrow, then? I thought you were a functional member of society."

"What does it matter? The guy doesn't want anything else in the house, and all this stuff will probably be trashed anyway." He gripped a large volume from a bottom shelf. "Here. This looks plenty old. I'll stick it in my bag. If this guy's sitting on millions, we're being underpaid. He's taking advantage of us."

Some things never change. Emma's cheeks tingled with anger.

Adam grabbed the door handle to the foyer and twisted. The metal latch rattled against the frame but refused to budge. He shook the latch and tried once more to crank it loose, but the door held firm. "Great. The damn door's stuck."

"*Someone* must not want you stealing *her* books. Take it as a sign."

"Ha! The latch probably just needs lube." He set the book on the reading desk and returned to the door. He gave the handle another firm twist, and it popped loose. "See, a little elbow grease did the trick." He returned for the book, but as he reached for it, a hardback tumbled from above, narrowly missing the back of his head and hitting the floor with a loud thud. "Hey!" He spun around. "What did you do that for? You could have killed me."

Emma looked at the gap in the shelf across the room where the book had been. "I didn't do anything." She pointed. "It fell from over there. The platform wiggles a little. Maybe it vibrated a book loose or something."

"That, or you want this magnificent library all to yourself. Fine, I'll leave the book here, but when you're trying to sell your first book and don't have enough money for ramen, remember we both could have been rich."

"I swear I didn't do anything."

"Sure, Em."

She turned toward the shelf and continued the search. "You're just scared you've pissed off the house. You don't want Rosalie coming back for you."

FOR SEVERAL DAYS, they spent every waking hour in the library, beginning after breakfast and ending when they couldn't keep their eyes open any longer. Emma brushed by books of all shapes, sizes, and types of binding —leather bound, cloth bound, and some that even looked as if they'd been bound in pigskin. Still, there were no books with faces.

Emma only stopped occasionally to flip through a book's pages. At first, she thought the books were versions of scripture, but as she looked at the pages, none of which were written in English, she realized that the pictures didn't reflect any of the Bible stories she'd heard as a kid. One showed a group of peasants drowning in a sea of fire as a demon-looking creature watched from the shore. Another showed a man hanging upside down as a snake-headed beast jabbed at his ribs with a sharp dagger. Across the pages, sneering creatures gathered to watch mortals suffer in front of them. Book after book seemed to focus on the monsters and contained countless images of beings with gnashing teeth and oddly proportioned features.

"I see why this chick lived out in the woods. My guess is she didn't have many friends," Emma said from midway up the stack one day as they were reaching the end of the collection.

Adam was still winding his way around the first floor. He'd never admit it, but Emma was certain he'd kept a slow pace to avoid having to climb the spiral staircase. He turned his book around and held up a picture of a half human, half goat. "Looks like that little dude who plays the flute."

"Pan?" She squinted. Emma had seen images like the one on that page. She searched the back of her mind for the name. "Baphomet. It's not Pan. I saw something on the news about it. Some satanic group wanted to put a bust of that thing outside a courthouse to protest a Ten Commandments statue. Something about the separation of church and state. The sage in the back is starting to make more sense. I think we've stumbled upon the house of a bona fide witch."

Adam's eyes widened. "You don't believe in that crap, do you?"

"I think it's all interesting, but I wouldn't say I *believe* it. But clearly, she did."

He tossed the book on the table and pulled out the next. "What do you think she used these books for?"

"I don't know. It would be helpful if we could understand any of them." She smirked. "Maybe it's just a bizarre collection. It must have taken decades to find all these."

After Emma had finished with the last book on the second floor, she climbed down the staircase. "No books with faces."

"Maybe we missed one."

"You shouldn't have missed anything. Took you days to finish the first floor. I know you were stalling."

Adam scratched the back of his neck. "Just being thorough."

Emma rubbed her eyes. "I've gotta get out of this house for a bit. All of this dust is killing my allergies, and I've been sneezing constantly."

Adam perked up. "It's a nice night. What if we barbecue? We've still got beer and hot dogs in the cooler, and I've got a little charcoal grill in my trunk. We could sit out front, get shit-faced, and relive our childhoods."

"What if we just stuck to the first two?"

Adam gave her a thumbs-up and disappeared through the library door. Emma scanned the room once more for any remaining hiding places. They'd combed the shelves, searched all the drawers, and even looked for loose stones in the wall, but the book was nowhere to be found.

As Adam grabbed his grilling supplies from the trunk, Emma carried the backyard patio chairs to the front porch. "Grab the cooler, would you?" he asked as he shut the trunk.

"Anything else, your highness?"

"A bottle opener," he replied with a smirk. Adam splashed lighter fluid on a stack of charcoal at the bottom of the tiny grill and tossed a match inside. As flame consumed the coals, he reached into the cooler, grabbed two beers, and handed one to Emma. "We should toast to a job well done."

She took the bottle opener from him. "A job well done? We haven't even found the book."

"Well, at least we've finished with the library."

"One massive room down, a dozen others to go. We'd be better off looking for a needle in a haystack."

Adam rolled his eyes. "Just be positive, would you?"

The sun set on the abnormally warm autumn evening as the smell of sizzling hot dogs filled the air.

"Remember when Dad made you go camping with us, and you stepped in poison ivy in the first hour of being in the woods?" he asked.

"And spent the rest of the weekend reading in the tent with puffy red legs—yes, yes, I do." She took a bite of hot dog. "Haven't been camping since."

"You're lucky. You know how many nights I spent freezing to death in the old tent and how many American-cheese sandwiches that man made me eat?" Adam leaned back in his chair. "You were sittin' pretty in your room while I was developing high cholesterol."

Emma laughed. "He loved it, though—being out there with you. You could see it on his face every time you two got home." Emma ran the toe of her sneaker along a mortar line in the porch. "You really ought to check in with them."

Adam crossed his arms. "I know. I just want everything to be right first. The insurance job is mine as long as I pass the certification test. I've been studying for weeks, but I don't want to say anything until I pass. Don't want to get their hopes up and then have this fall through. I never was a good test taker."

"But they'd just be happy to know you're okay and that you're giving it your best. That's all they want, I think. Hell, at this point, they just want to hear from you." Emma swirled the dregs of beer in the bottom of her bottle. "What if you come back with me after we find the book? You've got to head up that way to drop off the book, don't you? You could stay at my place for a few days. I don't have a ton of space, but the couch isn't half-bad, and we could go see Mom and Dad together. It'll be less pressure for you."

Adam fidgeted with his hoodie zipper. "You always were the rational one. I'll think about it."

Emma thought back to her argument with him, the one that he'd been so willing to overlook in the last few days. After a moment of silence, she cleared her throat. "I'm sorry I called you a failure."

His eyes darted up at her. "You mean a 'perpetual failure'?"

Emma avoided eye contact. "Yeah. I shouldn't have said it, and it's not even true. I was just pissed off."

Adam laughed just a little too loudly to be believable. "Oh, I know it's not true. But for what it's worth, I'm sorry I took so long to pay you back. My plan to make the extra money back fell through, and I barely had a place to live for a few weeks."

Emma locked eyes with him. "I didn't know that. You should have told me. I could have helped, or you could have stayed with me."

"Maybe, but..." Adam looked out across the yard.

"What is it?"

"Thought I saw headlights coming up over the hill."

Emma squinted. "I don't see anything. Maybe they're on the back road on the other side of the woods."

Adam pointed as a white glow grew brighter at the edge of the clearing. "No, look."

"You aren't expecting anyone, are you?"

"Nope. We're supposed to have the place to ourselves."

The glow intensified as a set of headlights appeared around the corner, shining through the bars in the gate.

She pushed up from her seat. "Should we go see who it is?"

Adam grabbed her arm. "No. No one else is supposed to be up here. Maybe it was a wrong turn. Just give it a minute, and see if they go away."

The car came to a stop in front of the gate.

"I feel awkward sitting here. We could at least see what they want." She waved at the pair of headlights. The car shifted on its high beams, and Emma shielded her eyes with her forearm.

"What's with the brights?" Adam asked. "Screw that guy. He's being a dick."

"Maybe it's the police or something. We don't want to cause any trouble."

The car switched off its lights and backed away from the gate. After a quick turnaround, it disappeared into the woods.

Adam slouched in his chair. "See? The guy probably just had the wrong address or got lost. Would you hand me another beer?"

CHAPTER FIVE

D*raaag. Thud.*

The sound pulled Emma from her last fleeting moments of sleep. She lay in her bed, irritated, and stared at the white plaster ceiling.

Draaag. Thud.

Shuffling followed the noise from the room above. *Maybe an animal?*

Draaag. Thud.

Emma pulled the covers back and slid her legs over the side of the bed as the sound came again. She looked at the ceiling once more. *It's definitely coming from upstairs. Maybe Adam being an ass?*

She tiptoed to the third-floor staircase and reached inside to find the light switch. The staircase light had burned out, but Emma could just make out the door at the top of the steps. She grabbed her phone from the writing desk and held its flashlight out into the darkness. Cobwebs lined the narrow staircase and got caught in her hair as she climbed.

She imagined the house's former owner walking up the stairs. Rosalie must have been short, a little under five feet, and hadn't bothered to clear the dusty webs that hung above her head.

When Emma reached the door at the top, she felt for a knob and twisted. "Locked," she said under her breath. She tried once more with additional vigor, but the door held firm. She pressed her ear against it and held her breath, hoping to hear the noise that had woken her.

"What are you doing up there?"

Emma's heart leapt as Adam called from the base of the stairs. She turned toward him and rushed down the staircase. "You scared the shit out of me."

"Sorry. I just came to ask what you wanted for breakfast."

"I'll grab something later. You don't know where the key to the third floor is, do you?"

"Nope," he replied. "Haven't made it up there yet."

"I heard noises coming from the ceiling of my bedroom. I think something might be in there."

"What noises?" Adam asked.

Emma slammed her heel on the ground and dragged it across the hardwood. "Like that."

Adam thought for a moment. "Probably just air in the

HOUSE OF SAGE AND SALT   53

radiators. I've heard it a few times." He shrugged. "These old houses always make weird noises. All this witch stuff getting to you, Em?"

Emma rubbed her temples. "Probably."

"I was thinking. We've spent the last few days buried in the library. We should take the day off, relax this morning, and maybe go for a walk in the woods or something this afternoon. I could use a good leg stretch."

"Great idea," Emma replied. "Maybe I'll crack open the laptop and see what flows."

He winked. "Just watch out for the mysterious tapping ghost."

Emma rolled her eyes.

"I'd better leave you to it, then," he said. "I'm sure whatever you come up with will be great. And since we've got no Wi-Fi, you shouldn't have trouble staying focused."

"In theory," she replied.

Although the story was slow to start, Emma had managed to carve out ten pages since arriving at the house. She'd sketched out a simple storyline in her mind, with sweet innocent Rosalie as the main character—a woman trapped in a house that was determined to consume her— but quickly tossed the idea after the first day in the library. The woman wasn't a victim or an involuntary hermit. She played a part in the house's darkness, only Emma hadn't yet figured out how.

Emma returned to her bedroom and checked the

power cable of her laptop. Even with the smallest wiggle, the charger would lose contact, resulting in a shutdown, thanks to a shoddy battery that could no longer hold a charge. She lifted the lid and pressed the power button. Nothing. She wiggled the power cord and wedged it tighter into the socket in the back of the laptop. Still nothing. She hit the power button with several successive taps. The plastic brick sat unflinching.

"You've got to be kidding me," she muttered as the blood left her fingers and her hands went ice-cold. The laptop had survived four years of undergrad work, countless papers, and intense exam study sessions, and now it had crapped out on her in the middle of nowhere and probably an hour away from the nearest electronics store.

It's just the battery, she told herself on loop as she tried to calm her breathing. *You've got most things backed up on a hard drive at home, and worst-case scenario, you can recreate what you've written so far.*

"Fine. Your days were numbered anyway. Once this is over, I'm replacing you, and I'm beating the shit out of you *Office Space* style. There's bound to be a notepad in this museum." She pulled open the drawers of the writing desk one by one but found nothing more than some old fabric and sewing supplies.

"You haven't seen any notepads around, have you?" She entered the living room. Adam lay on the couch with

HOUSE OF SAGE AND SALT   55

his headphones on and his eyes shut, so she continued the search solo.

Emma found a fountain pen and notepad in a drawer in the library desk, tucked under a magnifying glass and a bottle of ink. "I guess this will work."

She returned to the second-floor bedroom, but before she'd uncapped the fountain pen, a flash from the window caught her eye. As she looked down over the front yard, a black Cadillac pulled up the dirt road, its shiny chrome catching the sunlight. A man in a sleek black suit, short in stature and round in shape, emerged from the back seat. He had a bald spot so large that Emma could see it from the window—he covered it with a fedora as he approached. He stood awkwardly at the closed gate as if looking for a bell, then he pulled a letter from his pocket. Just as he was preparing to affix it to the wrought iron, he looked up at Emma's window. She stepped back, but he must have caught a glimpse, because he waved vigorously.

What now? She descended the staircase to the entryway and opened the front door. As she approached the mystery man, he pulled a handkerchief from his pocket and dabbed his sweaty forehead.

"So glad I caught you," he said as she reached the gate.

Emma put her hands on her hips. "Can I help you?"

"I heard a rumor that someone moved in up here." The man's gaze flashed uneasily between Emma and the house. "I just wanted to introduce myself and welcome you folks to town. My name is Theodore, and I'm the reverend of one of the local Rudder churches."

Great. A backwoods religious type. Just what I need. Emma shrank back from the gate. "Sorry, Theodore. We haven't had many visitors out this way. You caught me by surprise."

"People usually just call me Reverend." He met her hesitation with a smile. "Word travels fast around a small town like this." His eyes darted once more to the house as he shuffled uncomfortably. "This place has quite a history. Did you all just move in?"

"Oh, we're not moving in. Just helping the new owner find a few items. I guess he was related to the lady who died here. Say, you don't know her name, do you? Was it Rosalie?"

The Reverend looked as if he'd eaten a handful of earthworms. "That's it." He swallowed hard.

"Know anything about her? Seems like she wasn't very well liked around town."

He let out a nervous chuckle. "Can't say she was. I don't think anyone from town's even been inside the place, but I've heard stories. It seems like you all are doing all right up here, aren't you?"

"Just fine," she replied. "But by the look on your face, it sounds like those stories weren't very happy ones."

The Reverend looked down at his feet. "I don't want to

keep you, but if you want to know more, why don't you come over for dinner? Consider it my welcome gift."

Emma ran the toe of her shoe through the dirt as she contemplated all the ways to say no.

"Don't worry. I didn't come to convert you or anything like that. And don't let the whole *Reverend* thing scare you off. The church is accepting of all types. Live and let live, really. We'd really love to see you for dinner. No strings attached."

What does he mean by "all types"? Emma unclenched her fist. *Stop being a dick. He's trying to be nice, and a free dinner is a free dinner.* Emma pulled the gate open ever so slightly, leaving just enough room for her to squeeze through. "Nice to meet you, Reverend. I'm Emma." She extended her hand. "Let me check with my brother, and we'll let you know about dinner."

"Oh, wonderful." The Reverend's limp-fish handshake was made worse by his overly moisturized pudgy fingers. "And before I forget..." He held out the white envelope. "This is just a welcome card with my contact info. If you need anything, don't hesitate to give me a call."

"Nice to meet you, Reverend," she said, but he had already turned toward the car and reached for the handle. Emma could see the faint silhouette of the driver through the tinted windows and waved as the car pulled away. *Adam is going to kill me.*

As Emma turned toward the house, a figure caught her

eye in the third-floor window. A woman in gray stood against the paneled glass, staring down at her, her silver hair long, frizzy, and protruding from her head like a feather duster. Emma's blood ran cold. *She's still alive.*

Adam stood at the front door, waiting for her. "Who the hell was that guy?"

Emma pushed past him. "The woman's name *is* Rosalie, and I just saw her in the third-floor window." She set the card on the dining room table then hurried up the second-floor staircase.

"What? How's that possible? We haven't left the house in a few days. She couldn't have been up there this whole time." Adam was hot on her heels.

"I know what I saw. It looks like she's in rough shape." Emma reached the base of the narrow staircase to the third-floor bedroom and raced up the stairs. She jiggled the handle, but the door was still locked from the other side. "Ma'am!" she shouted as she knocked on the door. "Are you all right in there?"

Adam put his hand on her shoulder. "Uh, Emma. If she's still alive and holed up in there, technically, we're trespassing." He squeezed.

She turned toward him. "Knock it off. She's probably scared and might be hurt. I thought you said they found a body." She knocked once more, but no one replied.

"They did. At least, that's what the guy told me."

Adam gestured for her to move aside, and Emma side-stepped down the narrow staircase.

"I thought you said this guy was legit and showed you papers."

"He did! I wouldn't bring you out here if I thought we'd be in danger or breaking the law." He twisted the handle and lifted up on the frame. "Sometimes these get stuck when the weather changes."

"Or she's locked herself in." She knelt and pressed her eye against the keyhole. "I don't see anyone, but the room's a pigsty."

"I bet you could get to the roof through the library window and climb up on the balcony to take a peek."

Emma cocked her head. "Or I could grab the ladder next to the greenhouse and not fall to my death."

"That's an option, smartass."

With Adam's help, Emma brought the old wooden ladder to the front of the house and propped it against the box gutter. Adam stood at a distance as Emma's foot hit the first rung. "At least hold the ladder if you're too chicken to go up there yourself," she said. "And promise to call 911 if I go careening to my death."

He steadied the ladder. "The cellphone service out here is crap. If you go falling to your death, there's not much I'll be able to do about it. Please don't go killing your-self. How am I going to explain that to Mom and Dad?

They're already pissed it's been so long, and now I'll have to tell them their favorite child's dead."

She couldn't always tell when he was messing with her, but it was obvious when he *wasn't* kidding. When he tried to joke about a subject that mattered to him, a deep wrinkle always developed across his forehead.

"I'll be fine," she replied as she began to climb. *I'll be fine* continued to loop in her head as the distance between her and the ground grew. When she reached the roof, she carefully stepped onto the slate tiles and wedged her foot against the edge of the nearby chimney to steady herself. Although the roof was steep, her sneakers held firmly to the dry tiles as she worked her way toward the third-floor balcony. She gripped the edge of the wooden balcony and pulled herself up to the platform, using the metal railing as a stabilizer. Once she'd climbed up onto the ledge, she slung her leg to the other side of the railing and stepped over.

"Made it!" She let out a relieved breath as she peered at the ground below.

Adam looked up at her, and the wrinkle in his forehead had vanished. "Thank God."

The rotting deck floor crackled in protest under her feet. The balcony was bare except for a faded patio chair and a side table, on which sat a potted plant that looked like it had been dead for decades.

Emma stepped toward the window to peek inside,

avoiding the worst boards. It was made from inch-long glass squares held together by a curved wooden frame. Several of the small window panels were missing or cracked, letting in a breeze that fluttered the gray curtains lining either side of the room.

"Curtains. Maybe that's what I saw." She reached for the handle of the exterior door, but it was locked. She pressed her face against the glass and looked into the room on the other side. A tall four-poster bed was positioned in the center, with just enough space to prevent the tops from scraping the edges of the slanted ceiling. A fireplace sat at the far end of the room, next to a reading chair and an area rug. The furniture inside mimicked that in the rest of the house—old, wooden, and covered with an unreasonable amount of dust. Rubbish lined the corners of the room, and old plates with rotting food were stacked next to the bed. The faded fleur-de-lis wallpaper was streaked from air pockets and failing glue, and most of the strips had curled at the edges. There was no white-haired woman, though.

"Everything all right?" Adam shouted from below.

"Fine," she shouted back. "No signs of anyone. It's just an ordinary bedroom. Gross, but ordinary."

"Any books?"

"None." She scanned the room once more, but aside from garbage and old clothes, Emma saw no places for the mystery book to hide. She turned to face the front yard and braced herself against the autumn chill. She looked down the hill and into the forest beyond. Farmland faded into the distance on her left, and a clearing sat in the middle of the woods, perhaps a mile or so across the tree line in front of her. Smoke billowed from the clearing and dissipated into the clear sky.

How lonely she must have been. No neighbors for a mile at least. "What were you doing out here, all alone, for so long? Witchy things? You thought you were a witch, didn't you, like that weird girl in elementary school who cast a love spell over Steve Neuhaus. You're what happens to girls like that when they grow up. And the Reverend was afraid of you. But why?"

Hot breath pulsed on the back of her neck, sending tingles down her spine. Emma shot up and twisted around. No one waited for her.

"Are you coming?" Adam shouted from below.

Emma looked through the bedroom window one last time as the curtains fluttered then turned to climb down toward the ladder.

"Everything all right?" Adam asked as Emma's feet reached solid ground. "You're pale."

Emma shuddered. "Just cold up there is all." She rubbed the back of her neck. "I'm glad I've come back down to earth."

"What did you see?"

Emma hesitated. "Just a bedroom, nothing special."

"No old woman waiting up there with a butcher knife or anything like that?"

Emma avoided Adam's gaze. "If so, she's playing hide-and-seek."

"What's wrong?"

"This sounds crazy, but while I was waiting for you to come back with the ladder, I swear I felt someone breathing on me. It was probably just the breeze, or maybe heat coming through the broken glass, but it was hot. You know that feeling you get when you're being watched? But I didn't see anyone."

"Probably just your imagination," Adam replied. "These old houses have lots of weird energy. Considering all the creepy shit we've found, I'm surprised I'm not having nightmares."

Emma shuffled uncomfortably as she turned toward the front of the house. "Can we go into town tonight? This place is giving me the creeps. Maybe we could go see a movie?"

"And where do you expect to find a movie? I think we'll have to settle for the diner again."

"Agnes it is," she replied.

CHAPTER SIX

E mma found herself staring at Rosalie's house once more from the passenger seat of Adam's car as the moon slipped behind the peak of the third-floor roof. "Feels like it's watching us."

Adam cocked his head. "It does kinda look like it's got a face."

Emma looked down at her lap. "That's reassuring."

Adam's headlights cut through the rolling mist that crept across the yard.

"This place really has you freaked out, doesn't it?"

"You should have seen the Reverend's face when I asked about Rosalie. The guy could barely stand to look at the house and was in a hell of a hurry to leave. It just has me thinking…"

"Thinking what?" Adam cut the ignition.

"What if Rosalie never left?"

Adam snorted. "I told you, the lady's dead. They carried her gross soupy body out a while ago."

"I know, but what if she never left—her spirit, I mean."

"What, a ghost? Really? I thought you didn't believe in ghosts."

Emma played with the hem of her shirt. "I don't, or at least I didn't. I don't know—I'm just creeped out. And you have to admit, some pretty spooky stuff has happened since we moved in. The Reverend definitely came to warn us."

He scratched his stubbled chin. "Okay, let's say she's haunting this place. If she wanted to hurt us, don't you think she would have done it by now? She could have thrown you off the roof today."

"You're probably right." She slowly reached for the car door handle. "Let's just go inside before I change my mind."

"I found a few board games in one of the hall closets," Adam said as they approached the house. "Want to play a game?" His tone was guttural like a horror-movie voice-over.

She stopped short of the front steps, and the cold night air sent a shiver through her body. "Would you cut out the jokes for the night? I'm not in the mood."

Adam's smile faded. "Sorry, Em. I didn't mean anything by it."

She felt as if the house was swallowing her as she stepped through the foyer. "I'm beat. I may take a shower and check out for the evening."

"Solitaire it is," he replied with a slight hint of disappointment.

Goose bumps lingered on Emma's skin as she climbed the stairs to the second floor. She tossed her clothes on the bed, draped herself in a fresh towel, then stepped into the bathroom across the hall, eager to wash off the stench of the day. She tiptoed quickly across the cold tile to the bath mat. A line of rust ran from the tub faucet and slithered into the drain below. The metal knobs squealed as she twisted, and water spewed into the basin. She let it run until it warmed then lifted the shower knob and pulled the curtain closed. The warm water chased away the autumn chill that had followed her in from the hall. Emma held her head under the shower faucet and sighed. Despite the initial shock, she'd gotten used to the well-water smell.

Maybe Emma had been imagining things and the Reverend was just a superstitious nut, but she needed answers. The Reverend knew more than he was letting on, and the welcome dinner would give her the chance to pry more details out of him on the local lore.

The hinges of the bathroom door squeaked.

"Give me a minute," she said through the curtain. The house had several other bathrooms, but she and Adam had only bothered to clean one. The rest were covered in grunge and grime, and Emma wouldn't dare step inside any of them with bare feet.

A shadow slunk along the edge of the bathtub then slowly rose up the checkered curtain.

"I said, give me a minute."

The figure lingered in front of the curtain.

"What the hell's the matter with you? Get out! I told you, I'm not in the mood!" Emma punched the shower liner, and the shadow burst like a water balloon filled with black ink, its contents trickling down the curtain into the tub.

"What the hell?" She stepped out of the black puddle that swirled around her feet and flung the curtain aside. Steam flowed steadily through the room as she grabbed her towel and scrambled out of the tub.

Her heels pounded the tile as she raced toward the door and stuck her head into the hallway, looking each way before turning back toward the bathroom. As she took a step inside, she noticed a set of dewy footprints leading to the mirror, then to the bathtub. Emma's mouth went dry as she read the message scrawled on the fogged mirror.

Away.

Adam jolted awake when Emma barged into his bedroom, knocking the book straddling his chest to the ground. "What? What's the matter?" he slurred.

"Someone snuck up on me in the shower and wrote a message on the mirror. I think it's her, Adam. Rosalie is here, and she wants us to leave." Panicked tears streamed down her cheeks.

Emma stayed close to Adam as he approached the bathroom.

She pointed to the tile floor. "I saw footprints, but they're gone."

Adam looked down at her feet. "That would make sense. You're walking around in your bare feet."

"How do you explain the mirror, then?" Emma approached the mirror message, still visible as the steam billowed from the bathtub.

Adam's head snapped to the mirror, and his body stiffened. "I thought you were over the jokes for the night."

"I didn't do it, Adam. I swear."

Adam leaned over the tub and cut the running water then looked back at the message as it slowly faded.

Emma turned toward the door. "I think we ought to leave. I'm getting dressed." Not waiting for a reply, she marched to her bedroom and shut the door. She pulled on a pair of sweatpants and a hoodie then sat on the bed and ran her hands over her temples, pressing hard and trying to calm her racing heart.

A soft knock came from the other side of the door. "All right if I come in?"

"Yeah."

Adam sat on the bed next to her and rested his hand on her leg. "All right. I have to admit, I'm freaked the hell out right now, but we can't leave."

Emma swiped his hand away and locked eyes with him. "I just watched a shadow burst into pieces and wash down the drain. The town hates this place and won't come near it, some rando has us looking for a book with a face, and the house is filled with all sorts of weird stuff. Something dark's going on here, and I don't like it."

Adam bit his upper lip. "What do you want to do? Do you want to leave? I'd understand. But, Emma, this is ten grand we're talking about. I can't just get up and walk away. So there's some freaky stuff happening, but like I said before, don't you think the ghost would have hurt us by now if she wanted to?" The wrinkle in his forehead formed once more.

"You can't stay here by yourself." Emma looked down at her lap. "I'm not going to be held responsible if this house swallows you whole."

Adam snorted. "Then stay. We can get through this together. You should write this shit down. An exploding shower shadow—you can't make that kind of thing up." He leaned in and hugged her.

Emma bit a hangnail on her ring finger. "The Reverend invited us to dinner tomorrow. If you want me to stay, you'll go with me. He knows more about this house than he's letting on, and I want to know what we're dealing with."

Adam tried to pull away, but Emma refused to loosen her grip. "You're out of your mind." Adam squirmed. "Why didn't you tell me earlier? You know I won't take any religious bullshit. I'll be insufferable. Can't I just stay here and hang out with the old lady?"

"Promise me, or I pack a bag and leave right now."

"Fine," he said in a monotone voice. "But do I have to call him 'the Reverend'?"

"You'll call him whatever he wants to be called." Emma loosened her grip.

"Okay, but I won't be happy about it. At least promise me you won't go sneaking off into the night. I'm right down the hall if you need me." He stood and walked to the bedroom door.

"See you in the morning," she said.

Once he'd disappeared around the corner, Emma rushed to the door and flipped the latch, although she wasn't sure what exactly she was trying to keep out and whether a simple lock would stop it. Her finger lingered over the light switch, but she couldn't bring herself to press it.

Later that night, she lay awake, listening to the creaks and groans of the house until she couldn't take it anymore.

Channel the energy, she thought, spotting the notebook and fountain pen at her writing desk. She switched on the desk lamp and pulled out the uncomfortable wooden chair.

Emma stared at the blank page of her notebook and took a few practice strokes across the page. The pain of losing her first few pages still lingered. She looked out onto the yard covered with a misty layer of moonlight then put her pen to paper.

Paramedics wheeled the stretcher across the uneven gravel, the aluminum frame jerking in their hands as they approached the ambulance. The breeze caught the sheet covering the body, revealing the woman's withered hand underneath. The house watched the scene unfold and wondered if the woman would ever come back. It needed her.

Emma sat back from the desk and reread her rough sentences. In theory, writing a horror novel in a creepy house was a great idea, but in practice, it freaked her out. She flipped back through the filled pages of the notebook, passing sketches and notes the woman must have taken from the countless books in the library. Most of the notes were gibberish and appeared to have been copied directly from the tomes in languages Emma couldn't understand. The woman had also recreated a few sketches, apparently focusing on evil beasts of personal interest.

Emma's eyes flashed to the portrait of Rosalie staring

down at her with an unflinching gaze. She closed the note-book and pushed away from the writing desk. After pulling the picture down, she set it out in the hallway and dragged a wooden chair to the door of the third-floor bedroom. With one swift motion, Emma wedged the chair under the doorknob.

CHAPTER SEVEN

A dam leaned against the back of the couch and scratched his forehead. "So we're really going to do this?"

Emma walked toward the front window and looked out into the yard. The Reverend's Cadillac was sprawled across the entrance to the wrought-iron gate, and the Reverend leaned patiently against the car. "He's waiting for us. You want me to stay until we find the book, don't you? Let's see if he can help."

"Fine. Let's just go before I change my mind."

Emma grabbed Adam by his shoulders. "But you can't be an asshole. Act like you want to be there. You can pretend for a few hours, can't you?"

Adam took his index fingers and dug them into the corners of his mouth, forcing his expression into a smile and speaking through his teeth. "Of course. I wouldn't dream of making it awkward for you."

"He seemed like a friendly guy. You might even like him." She opened the front door and waved at the Reverend.

"Doubtful," he replied as he followed close behind.

"Hi, Reverend," Emma said as she approached. "Sorry, we should have opened the gate for you."

The Reverend held up his hands. "No need to apologize. I'm just glad you two could join. Good to see you again, Emma."

Adam pulled the gate open and stepped toward him.

"And this must be your brother." The Reverend extended his hand.

Adam gripped the Reverend's hand and gave it a comical shake. "Adam."

"A pleasure to meet you, Adam. We'd better get going."

The driver held the door for the trio as they climbed into the rear of the Cadillac. The back had been hollowed out and lined with a wraparound leather couch.

"Nice car, Reverend. Donations sure go a long way, don't they?" Adam asked with a grin.

Emma jabbed him in the ribs as her cheeks went hot.

The Reverend laughed off the comment. "You should see my helicopter."

Adam's eyes widened.

"Just kidding, of course. All donations go straight back to the church and improving the lives of its members. If I take anything from the church, it's a modest salary."

The Cadillac struggled to make the winding turns on the wooded road. "Drink?" The Reverend reached for a decanter perched in a built-in minibar.

"Reverends can drink?" Adam asked.

The Reverend poured three crystal glasses of amber liquid. "Temperance only applies to a few religions, and fortunately for me, my church doesn't require it."

"I mean, as long as you call it the blood of Christ, anything goes, right?" Adam smirked.

"Many believe the wine does become the blood of Christ during communion, so if you believe such a thing, you technically wouldn't be consuming any alcohol at all." He passed glasses to his guests then aimed the rim of his glass in Adam's direction. "To new friends."

Emma tilted her glass back and sipped. Wine aside, she wasn't much of a drinker, and she coughed as the burn hit the back of her throat. Adam shrugged and emptied the glass with a single gulp.

When the limo reached the edge of the woods, the driver turned right, taking the road away from town. "We're not going into town, then?" Emma asked.

"Oh, no. I'm a fan of the diner as much as the next, but I thought something home-cooked might be in order." The

Reverend cracked the back windows, and corn stalks whizzed by on the left, filling the car with a sea of white noise as the wind blew through them. "That sound never gets old."

"Did you grow up here?" Emma asked.

The Reverend shook his head. "I'm a city boy at heart, but I go wherever I've been called to serve. I've taken quite a liking to this little town, though."

The car passed a clearing in the stalks, and Emma got a glimpse of just how far the fields extended. Eventually, the rows of corn ended and were replaced by barren plowed earth. A hodgepodge of metal buildings sat in the distance behind the fields, forming an obscure skyline that sat in odd contrast to the country landscape.

"You see those buildings over there?" the Reverend asked. "That's the tail end of the old manufacturing park. When the markets crashed in 2008, the factories went belly-up. The town's never been the same since. It's—"

"A ghost town," Adam said from behind his second tumbler.

The Reverend nodded. "So I thought, why not make the most of a bad situation? We have the buildings—let's put some of them to use. The church bought a few of the salvageable buildings a few years back, and we're putting the finishing touches on the sanctuary as we speak."

The driver took another right about a mile down the road. Emma perked up in her seat as the car pulled through the trees to a large open clearing. "I recognize this. I could see the clearing from the third floor of the house."

A one-floor mid-century modern home sat against a backdrop of orange and yellow leaves. The left side of the house held a living room enclosed by large glass walls, while the right was made from thick layers of poured concrete. A woman stood at the front door, her bleached-blond bob glistening under the porch lights as she waved.

The Reverend polished off his tumbler. "There's the wife. She's very excited to meet you."

"Hell of a house, Reverend." Adam gawked at the imposing structure. "Sorry, I meant *heck*."

The Reverend chuckled. "No need to apologize."

As the driver pulled the car alongside the house and opened the rear door, the Reverend's wife waved to them. "You must be Adam and Emma. I'm Yvonne. So nice to meet you."

"Nice to meet you too," Emma replied.

Yvonne gestured for them to follow. "Dinner's almost ready, so come on inside."

The interior of the Reverend's house was just as impressive as the outside. A long leather couch stretched across the living room, and a large cement fireplace sat opposite. The living room bled into an open-concept dining room and kitchen. A cook in a white apron leaned over the gas range, and the smell of roasting meat filled the air.

Yvonne led them to the center of the stark dining room with a large table made from a single piece of heavy stained oak. It was bordered by a set of modernist chairs with lime-green fabric. Emma took a seat next to Adam. The chandelier overhead was made of several inverted glass jars with Edison lights screwed into each and cast a warm glow over the room.

Yvonne rounded the table. "Something to drink? Beer? Wine?"

"Uh, beer would be fine," Adam replied.

"Give him one of those local brews, hon," the Reverend added. "The IPA's a good one."

"Coming right up." She turned toward Emma. "And for you?"

"Do you have red wine?"

"I love a good cabernet," she replied. "We've got a few bottles lying around. And the usual for you, dear?"

"Sounds great." The Reverend squeezed Adam on the shoulder. "I'm going to wash up. You two make yourselves as home."

Once the Reverend was out of earshot, Adam whispered, "This is nuts. We're in the middle of nowhere. He's got to be one of those multimillionaire TV reverends, right?"

Emma looked up at the thick wood beams running along the ceiling and the paneled skylights. "I don't know. This place *is* pretty impressive."

"Wonder if they'll try to sell us on a religious time-share or something. I bet the whole thing is a pyramid scheme. These things usually are. That, or we'll get Kool-Aid pie for dessert."

"What's this about Kool-Aid?" the Reverend asked as he returned to the dining room.

Emma felt a rush of blood settle in her cheeks.

"Oh, nothing." Adam shuffled uncomfortably in his chair.

"This place does seem a little lavish, doesn't it?" the Reverend said.

Did he hear the whole thing? Emma wondered. "We're sorry, this is just—"

"Please. You don't have to apologize. And don't worry —we're not trying to convert you. We couldn't even if we wanted to. No, our faith requires that you come to it willingly. We just want to ensure that you enjoy your stay here." The Reverend rounded the table and took a seat across from them as his wife returned with drinks.

"I'm sorry," Adam said, "but I've got to call bullshit. When we drove through the town the other day, the place looked like a war zone. The streets are crumbling, and most places are out of business. How can you justify this while the town is in ruins?"

Emma grabbed her wineglass and took a large gulp.

The Reverend laughed. "I have to admit, you're right, Adam." He leaned in and took a sip from his old-fashioned.

"When I came to town a few years back, it was truly in ruins. The manufacturing plants had closed their doors—plants that employed three quarters of the town, mind you—and the growing season had been catastrophic. Rudder was out of money, but with that came an interesting opportunity. Our church has been blessed with an influx of cash from our generous members, and I saw a chance to help while building a place for my people to gather. The land was cheap, we needed more space, and this seemed like the perfect opportunity to solve our problems and help the town."

"How big is your congregation?" Emma asked, trying to ease the tension.

"A few thousand," he replied.

"Thousand?" Adam gave Emma a smug smirk.

"The majority come in from out of town for the weekend service," the Reverend added. "It's quite an influx of customers for the local businesses, and the town's in talks for a big revitalization project." The Reverend swirled his drink. "I'm getting the sense that you haven't had great experiences with religion."

"You could say that," Adam replied.

Emma clenched her jaw. "We grew up Catholic. Adam never recovered, apparently." She gritted her teeth. "But that's no reason for him to be rude."

The Reverend's smile grew wide. "Well, that explains it. I was starting to think it was me." He held up the back of his hand. "When I was a kid, they used to whap us across the knuckles. Just be glad that was before your time."

Adam's expression softened. "Rev, maybe I haven't given you enough credit."

"Enough about me. What about the two of you?" the Reverend asked. "Tell me about yourselves."

Emma and Adam looked at each other, neither wanting to be the first to speak.

Adam leaned in. "My sis is an aspiring writer, aren't you, Em?"

"You could say that," she replied. "Emphasis on *aspiring*, I guess."

"Ah, perhaps a case of writer's block? I'm familiar with that ailment," the Reverend said.

Emma smiled. "On the nose. I managed a few pages for my novel, then my computer died."

The Reverend sipped from his glass once more then leaned in again. "A novel? How wonderful. What subject?"

Emma waffled. "Horror."

"Horror? I suppose you've read the greats, then— Shirley Jackson, Lovecraft, and Stephen King, one of my personal favorites."

"Of course!" Emma perked up. "I'm surprised you're familiar."

"I read them all as a boy. Can't say I have much time for reading now, but I remember them fondly."

The chef approached the table with an armful of plates. "I'm sorry to interrupt."

The Reverend beamed as he ogled the plate in front of him. "I hope you like Italian. Winnie's oxtail is my favorite, but she's also made short-rib stuffed ravioli and veal scaloppini for us tonight. I hope you don't have any reservations about veal."

Yvonne joined them at the table and slid a fresh cocktail over to the Reverend.

He pecked her on the cheek. "You're too good to me."

Emma forked a ravioli.

"Decadent, aren't they?" the Reverend asked as she took a bite.

"It's one of the best things I've ever eaten," she replied.

"It's a nice break from sandwiches and hot dogs," Adam added as he sliced a piece of veal.

At first, Emma had been eager to bring up the house, but she found dinner with the Reverend so much of a welcome distraction she couldn't bring herself to put a damper on the jovial mood. Later that evening, once all four of them had pushed their empty plates toward the center of the table, Emma picked at her cuticles as she worked up the nerve to bring up the house. "Reverend?"

The Reverend was leaning back in his chair, nursing a full stomach. "Yes, dear?"

Emma put her elbows on the table. "When you

stopped by the other day, you mentioned you'd heard stories about the house. What kind of stories?"

His eyes flicked toward her. "Dark ones. I suppose you've found a few artifacts—some that might be hard to explain or understand."

"That's an understatement," Adam replied.

"Really?" The Reverend scooted his chair up to the table. "What have you found?"

Emma thought of the white-haired woman in the window. "Not so much *what* but *who*."

The Reverend scrunched his bushy eyebrows. "Who?"

"Rosalie. I know this sounds crazy, but I think I've seen her. I've felt her, too, like she's following me—her spirit, I mean." Emma shrank back in her chair. "I think she wants us out."

"I see." The Reverend leaned in and met Emma's gaze. "When we met, you mentioned the new owner had hired you to find a few items. What kind of items?"

"Just one. A book."

Adam kicked Emma in the shin.

"What?" She elbowed him back. "We might as well tell him." She met the Reverend's gaze once more. "Her house is full of books with pictures of demons and all sorts of weird creatures. Reverend, what do you know about Rosalie? You're keeping something from us."

The Reverend rubbed his chin. "Supposedly, she was in possession of a special book of sorts."

"Oh?" Goose bumps traveled up Emma's arms.

The Reverend looked down at his lap. "You might think this silly, but it's believed that house harbors a book of dark magic—a book of the devil. I know, it sounds absurd —a book of demons. I thought the idea was crazy, too, the first time I heard of such a thing."

"What exactly does a book of dark magic look like?" Adam asked.

"No one knows for sure, but I'd guess big, dense, and potentially covered with human flesh. That's the rumor, at least." The last bit made his voice waver.

Emma felt the acidic tomato sauce burbling up her esophagus. "Human flesh?"

"It might sound morbid, but books like that exist, even nonmagical ones." He locked eyes with Emma. "You haven't found such a book, have you?"

"Nope," Adam shot back before Emma had a chance to speak.

"But if we do find it, the new owner promised us a reward to retrieve it," Emma added.

The Reverend sat straight up in his chair. "Oh no. That would be a terrible mistake."

"Then what do you propose we do with it?" Adam asked. "Burn it?"

The Reverend shot a worried glance at his wife. "You could try, but a book like that wouldn't burn. Keep it closed, and call me. We would have to find a place to put it where it would never again see the light of day."

"And I don't suppose you'd be willing to pay us ten grand?"

The Reverend's expression soured. "How do you know the person who hired you?"

"I don't directly, but—"

He folded his hands. "And I don't suppose you find it odd that a stranger would offer you so much money to find a book?"

"That's what I've been saying the whole time," Emma said.

"This person put you in grave danger. And that book in the wrong hands could cause a lot of harm, not just to you or the town but possibly to the entire world."

Yvonne rested her hand on her husband's. "You're scaring them, dear."

The Reverend's expression softened. "I'm sorry. That wasn't my intent."

Emma tried to steady her trembling hands by holding onto the table. "We should leave then—just pack up our bags and go."

The Reverend reached across the table and grabbed her hand. "You certainly could."

"We only have a room or two left to search. We've been through the entire library. We could finish the place off if we stayed another day," Adam said.

Emma's eyes widened. "We can't stay. You heard the Reverend. We're in danger."

"If this book really is so powerful, don't you want to find it? Don't you want to make sure that we leave it in safe hands?" Adam stood from the table. "If we're going to flush ten grand down the drain, we ought to at least do something great, Em. If the guy that hired us is planning to use the book, shouldn't we put a stop to it?"

Emma's hand shook as she reached for her wineglass and tipped it back against her lips. She'd been so eager to save herself that she hadn't considered what would happen if they left the book behind. Surely, someone would find it eventually. And if it fell into the wrong hands... "You're right. If the book is dangerous, we ought to find it and make sure it's out of circulation. It's the right thing to do." She stood next to her brother.

Yvonne looked up at her, worried. "Are you sure?"

Emma took a deep breath. "So far, all Rosalie's managed to do is make some noise and write a creepy message on the mirror."

"If the woman's spirit still resides in the house, and she knows you're looking for the book... let's just say, the more determined she is to stop you, the less innocuous she'll be," the Reverend replied.

Emma looked over at Adam. "We can handle it, right?"

"If you're in, I'm in," he replied.

"Then I think it's time we head back to the house. We have work to do."

Emma's stomach churned as they returned to the Reverend's car. As the Cadillac wound its way through the woods and reached the wrought-iron gates, Emma felt more and more uneasy.

The Reverend reached for her arm as the driver opened the rear door. "I would be remiss if I didn't warn you again of the substantial danger that opening one of these books may pose." The Reverend shifted in his seat, and a bead of sweat formed on his forehead. "These books are powerful and can cause unimaginable harm in the wrong hands."

"Just be ready for us when we find it." Emma's voice wavered.

"I'll be ready. And if you run into trouble, I'm just a phone call away."

"Not coming in, Reverend?" Adam asked.

The Reverend pulled a handkerchief from his pocket and wiped his brow. "I haven't ever set foot in that house, and I plan to keep it that way. I hope you understand."

Once the car had turned around and pulled down the drive, Emma and Adam faced the house in the darkness. Adam rested his hand on her shoulder. "Are you sure you want to do this, Em? If you want to grab your bag and go, I completely understand."

"And let you have all the fun and come out a hero? No way."

"You sure?"

She leaned her head against him. "I have no freaking clue what's going on right now, but I know this is the right thing to do. We'll spend one more night in the house, find the book, and get the hell out of here. And Rosalie will just have to deal with it."

CHAPTER EIGHT

The sound of clanking pots and pans rattled Emma awake. "Do you hear that?" She rolled to the edge of the mattress and peeked over onto the floor. The covers on the makeshift bed where Adam slept were pulled back, and Adam was nowhere to be found. After the dinner with the Reverend, Emma had been too freaked out to sleep, and Adam had kindly sacrificed his bed and back so that they could sleep in the same room. She climbed out of bed and followed the source of the sound through the hallway and down to the kitchen.

Adam stood over a sizzling frying pan. "About time you're up. I'm surprised you even slept at all. I've been up since five. I've already double-checked the entire first floor. Every drawer, every crack, and every crevice. I thought I would give us a head start."

Emma scowled as she took a seat at the small dine-in table. "I assume you're well caffeinated."

He nodded rapidly. "A whole pot's worth. Now, come on! First, breakfast, then we need to get going if we want to tackle the basement."

She looked down at her lap. "All right, as long as you promise no more coffee—you're giving me anxiety. And why are you so excited? Didn't you hear anything the Reverend said last night?"

Adam rounded the table and set a steaming plate and coffee cup in front of her. "I heard everything. The whole thing's crazy, but how often do you have the chance to find an evil book of magic? Why aren't you excited?"

Emma flipped her wrist. "Oh, I'm just concerned about a ghost murdering us is all. Any other interesting finds in your search this morning?"

"Nothing. You'd think in a place with books about demons, we'd at least find a Ouija board or some Tarot cards. All I found was dusty silverware and useless junk."

"You don't think real witches use Ouija boards, do you?"

"No, I'm just saying I'd expected to find *something* aside from the books in the library."

Emma ate as quickly as possible. As soon as she'd taken her final bite, Adam jumped from the table and took their plates to the sink. "I'll wash them later. Time for the basement!"

Emma slunk out of her chair. "You're handling last night's news a bit better than I am."

"How often do you get to save the world?"

"But aren't you just a little scared?" She rubbed her arms to chase away the chill.

"Terrified. But a few days ago, I was terrified of being horribly ordinary. So this is a nice change of pace."

Emma chuckled. Despite how absurd it sounded at first, Adam's reasoning resonated.

The edge of the basement door ground against the frame as he forced it open. "Maybe the old bat locked little children down here Hansel and Gretel style."

The rickety basement steps faded into the darkness below. Emma pressed the button on the staircase wall, but the darkness remained. "She wasn't very good at changing light bulbs. I don't suppose you found a flashlight or two lying around."

"I've got a few in the trunk. Be right back." Adam disappeared into the kitchen.

Emma teetered on the edge of the top step, trying to get a glimpse of the basement below. A whiff of damp earth carried up the stairs. *All basements smell the same.*

He returned with two flashlights and handed one to Emma. He pointed his flashlight toward the bottom of the basement steps. The stairs led to a stone floor below, and as they descended, Emma felt condensation form on her skin.

A creature scurried against the far wall, and Emma

aimed her beam in its direction. Nothing. "Of course, we saved one of the worst parts of the house for last."

They swept their flashlights across the dusty floor at the bottom of the steps. Dew glistened on the rock wall foundation where the white plaster had broken away, exposing the raw stone underneath. Small piles of plaster crumbles accumulated at the foundation's corners. Three storage crates lined the far-right wall, draped by a large white sheet. Adam crossed the room and pulled the cover away.

Emma backed against a wall out of fear that something might slink from the darkness and sneak up behind her. "I don't think she'd keep the book down here. It would probably mold with all this moisture."

As Adam leaned in and lifted the lid of the first crate, he held his arm to his nose.

"What?"

"Mothballs." He set the lid aside and reached in. "Just a bunch of old clothing. You're right—this place is kinda gross for such a valuable book."

Emma aimed her flashlight at the other end of the basement, behind the staircase. "Looks like there's another door down that way."

Adam rose to his feet, and they crept farther into the basement's depths, past covered furniture and a hodge-podge of storage boxes. A small arched doorway sat at the far end of the room, leading to a narrow stone staircase that cut down into the foundation.

Adam held the flashlight under his chin as if he were telling a ghost story. "Must be where she hides the bodies."

"Knock it off." Emma shined her flashlight down the staircase. The steps wound around, making it impossible to see what awaited them at the bottom. She took the first one, with Adam close behind, but these steps were shorter than most, and her heel caught the second one abruptly. She fell forward, but Adam grabbed her arm and pulled her back.

"Careful there."

Emma steadied herself and continued the descent. When she reached the bottom of the steps, a thick wooden door sat in her way, and a crosshatched barred window gave a glimpse into the room beyond. She looked down at the handle and cradled the rusted padlock in her hands. "Locked." Her voice echoed up the staircase. "I thought I saw a key ring with a few weird-looking keys hanging next to the top of the stairs. Maybe one'll fit it."

Adam put his hands on her shoulders. "It's worth a shot. I'll grab them." Adam's sneakers scraped against the stone steps as he climbed, and his footsteps trailed off as he crossed the basement to the staircase.

Emma held the flashlight up to the metal-grated window and pressed her face against it. The light cast a grid pattern on the far wall and a small altar tucked against it. The lens of her flashlight hit the metal and flickered.

"Shit, shit, shit," she said under her breath as the light died altogether. She tapped the flashlight frantically. The light flickered and stuttered back to life. As she lifted it to the window, her eyes met someone else's.

A head sat framed in the window, gray and rotting in the yellow glow of Emma's flashlight. Clumps of wild white hair hung in front of the woman's face. Putrid pale patches speckled her thin cheeks, and her skin sagged as if it had outgrown her skull.

Emma sucked in the cool basement air and filled her nose with the smell of decay and rot as she fell against the stairs. The woman opened her mouth to speak, revealing a set of jagged yellow teeth that hung past her lips, lined with green decay. Her voice came as a raspy whisper at first, as if she hadn't used it in a hundred years. "Away."

Emma felt her heart thump behind her eyes. She wanted to run, needed to run, but something held her there. "Where is the book?" Her voice was weak and barely audible.

"Away," the woman said again, her fetid breath wafting through the air and burning Emma's nostrils.

"I—"

"Away, away, away," the woman began to chant. Emma backed up the spiral staircase one step at a time until the woman's whisper became a full-blown scream. "Away!"

The flashlight pulsed and died, and Emma let out a bloodcurdling scream as she scampered up the remaining stairs. She ran through the dark, twisting past old furniture and knocking her shins on storage boxes. As she reached the staircase to the first floor, Adam met her, and the beam from his flashlight blinded her.

"What happened? Are you okay?" he asked.

"I saw her. She's in that room."

"Well, I found a set of keys that looks promising. Sounds like she doesn't want us finding out what's in that room."

Emma willed her feet to turn around and follow her brother, but they seemed fused to the ground.

Adam grabbed her by the arm. "Stay behind me."

Emma's short breaths came in rapid succession as she held close to her brother. He descended the staircase and disappeared around the corner as Emma stood glued to the top step. She held her breath as a gasp and a heavy metallic *thunk* came from below.

"Oh God!" she shouted as she rushed down the stairs. When she reached the arched doorway, she slid down the steps and onto the earthen floor, her body kicking up a cloud of dirt and dust. She scrambled to her feet. "Are you okay?"

"This room reeks." He spun around and blinded her with his flashlight.

Emma put her hands on her knees and tried to catch her breath.

He held the heavy padlock in his hand. "Look, it's okay. No one's here. What do you think this room is for?" He strolled to the far wall as Emma regained her composure and pushed herself to her feet.

Adam shined his flashlight at a set of several recessed shelves, each with a wooden box tucked inside. "Look at this."

Emma backed toward the doorway. "Adam, I think those are coffins. This place is a tomb. Get away from there."

Adam's mouth hung open as he cautiously approached the wall and rested his palm on one of the boxes. "You don't think she would have put the book in one of these, do you?"

"No way. If that book's so important, she wouldn't bury it down here. She would have kept it close to her." Emma's heel hit the first step. "Can we please go back upstairs? I don't like it down here."

Adam turned and scanned the rest of the room with his flashlight. "There are at least a dozen other coffins here. What kind of house has its own crypt?"

"I don't know. Look, to be honest, I really don't even care. Can we please just go back upstairs? The book isn't down here, and I need to get out of this basement. Please?" Her voice cracked.

He stepped toward her. "Let's go. If it's in one of these coffins, the old bat can keep it, for all I care. I don't want to know what's inside."

Emma felt light-headed as she followed closely behind her brother. The walls seemed to pulse as if the house were breathing.

"So, no books to speak of in the basement. We've cleared the library and the foyer, so the third floor's all that's left," Adam said.

Emma gripped the handrail of the staircase leading up to the ground floor. "She would have kept it close to her. It's got to be on the third floor. That room was such a mess. Maybe I overlooked it." Once they reached the safety of the first floor, Emma grimaced. "I don't know that I can take much more of this house."

"So let's find the book and bolt!"

Emma straightened her stance. "You don't think one of those keys will work on the third-floor bedroom, do you?"

Adam held up the key ring. "These are all too thick. Maybe we can try to pry the door open or break the glass from the outside."

"Might be our only option unless we can convince Rosalie to open it for us. I saw some tools in the shed out back. Let's make our own key then get the hell out of here."

CHAPTER NINE

E mma's hand was cold and clammy as she clenched the handle of a rusty hatchet.

"A little aggressive, don't you think?" Adam asked.

"Maybe, but do you have any better ideas?"

"It wasn't an insult. I'm just so proud to see my sister breaking and entering with such style."

Emma twisted the glass knob to Rosalie's bedroom. She swore it felt as if someone was holding the door firmly from the other side. A shadow swayed under the crack in the door, and she stepped back toward the stairs, nearly slipping on the top step before Adam held her back.

"What's wrong?" he asked.

She pointed at the bottom of the door. "Someone's on the other side."

Adam's eyes darted to the floor. "I see it." He put his

hand on her back. "Are you sure you don't want me to go first?"

Emma swallowed hard. "No, I've got it." She lifted the hatchet and aimed at the wood surrounding the door handle. "Just tell me we're doing the right thing—that it's worth the risk."

"I can't say for sure, but keeping a book of dark magic out of the wrong hands sounds like the right thing to do. If only our parents had prepared us for such a dilemma."

"You'll always be a smartass, won't you?"

"Would you want me to be any other way?" he asked.

"I love you, Adam."

"I love you too, Em."

Emma brought the hatchet down hard on the wood just next to the doorknob plate. A few strikes missed their mark and bounced off metal, but as Emma pounded the door with the hatchet over and over again, wood began to chip away. After a few dozen strikes, she turned to Adam. "Your turn. It's harder than I thought. Jack Torrance made this look easy."

Adam hacked at the door and frame, slowly revealing the lock mechanism as the wood chipped away. After another dozen whacks, he stepped back to admire his work. "Ready?"

"For what?" Emma asked.

With a swift kick, Adam hammered his foot against the door, and it swung open into the room beyond as the lock twisted sideways and broke free from the frame. As Emma stepped through the doorway behind him, an arctic chill greeted her along with the putrid smell of rotting food. Sunlight caught the dust motes floating through the air. Emma stepped farther into the room, but Rosalie wasn't there to greet her. Her eyes traced the floor, which was spattered with dirty dishes and remnants of rotting food leading up to the four-poster bed.

Adam pointed at the bed, where a large brownish-black stain saturated the center of a faded white comforter —body fluid soaked into a worn indent, no doubt where a corpse once lay. "This must be where the old lady kicked it."

Emma looked on with morbid curiosity but refused to move closer.

"She must have been here so long she liquefied," Adam said. "Can you imagine that deliveryman finding this? What a nightmare."

"They didn't even bother cleaning up the mess when they took the body? How did he even get in if the door was locked?"

"Looks like Rosalie's playing tricks on us. No wonder she haunts the place. I'd be pissed, too, if I went like this."

"How can you stand that smell?" She gagged.

Adam crossed the room to the balcony door and pushed it open.

"It wasn't locked?" Emma asked.

"Nope. Now we've got a cross breeze to clear out the stink."

Emma shivered as she turned toward the fireplace, where a row of pictures lined the mantel. She lifted one of the heavy brass frames to examine the family posed in front of the very house in which she stood. "Come look at this."

Adam peered over her shoulder.

She held out the picture frame. "It must be her family." She squinted at the grainy row of children. "This picture's old. She's probably one of the kids."

"I bet the whole family was messed up." He slid a box of extended matches from the dusty mantel and knelt next to the fireplace. "I'll light a fire if you want to start the search. It's fucking freezing in here." He turned toward her. "You don't think those coffins we found in the basement were..."

She counted the figures in the picture. "There were at least a dozen coffins, and there are only five people here."

Emma walked the perimeter of the room to the window, taking inventory of any places the woman might have hidden the book and avoiding the bed altogether. The scene below was serene, in stark contrast to the situation inside. *I'd be pissed too.* She thought of Adam's words and imagined what it must have been like to die alone in a room full of filth, with no family or friends to speak of.

The hairs on her arms stood on end as a static cling

filled the room. The glass in front of her had fogged from her breath, and she watched in horror as another patch fogged next to it. Emma spun around, but no one stood between her and Adam, who was still crouched in front of the fireplace. Rosalie had been quiet, but the witch was definitely watching.

As the logs caught, smoke rolled out over the edge of the fireplace and along the mantel until it collected against the ceiling. Emma backed toward the balcony door. "The fire's putting off an awful lot of smoke. Is that normal?"

Adam waved the smoke away from his face. "Nope, not normal. I'll grab some water."

He rushed from the room and returned a few minutes later with a bucket. As water hit the flames, the logs hissed and cracked and let off a hot burst of smoke and steam that filled the room. Once the smoke had dissipated a bit, Adam moved close to the mantel and reached inside. A stack of blackened objects fell free from the flue in a cloud of smoke and soot that momentarily consumed him.

"What the hell?" He reached into the fireplace once more and pulled an object free from the stack, holding it up to get a better look.

"What is it?"

"I think it's a shoe." He pulled a leather flap loose from the flattened form and ran his finders along a string running through a small set of holes. "These are the laces."

"That's freaking creepy. Why would she be stashing

shoes up there?" Emma stepped toward the fireplace and knelt to look inside. "There must be ten pairs here."

"Maybe her victims. Looks like they're all different sizes. What the hell was she doing in this place?"

Emma shuddered. "I'm not sure I want to know the answer to that question. But if she's got shoes stuffed up her chimney, what else is she hiding in this room?"

Adam looked down at the area rug. "Maybe we're standing on it."

They moved aside the furniture sitting atop the rug, which they then rolled up from one end.

"Any other theories?" Emma stared at an ordinary hardwood floor. She traced the room with her eyes, settling on a loose piece of wallpaper whose edges fluttered in the cold breeze. She approached and ran her hand along the wall, smoothing out the paper and pressing it back into place. The piece detached once more, and she gripped it by its sides and yanked.

"You've chosen a terrible time to redecorate," Adam said.

"Would you shut up and give me a hand? I can't reach the top corner."

Adam crossed the room and helped pull the strip free. They worked together, leaving only several small patches where the adhesive still clung anemically.

Adam's eyes traced the sloppy black paint strokes covering the wall. "This is messed up."

Emma had seen the symbol many times before but only in horror movies. "A pentagram." A knot formed in her stomach. She approached another loose piece of wall-paper and pulled, revealing another circled star underneath.

"I wonder..." Adam turned toward the bed and knelt, putting his palms on the floor but not touching his face to the dirty hardwood. "Help me move the bed."

"No freaking way. I'm not going near that puddle of gross."

"You don't have to touch it—just grab a leg and pull."

Emma stepped toward the edge of the bed and tried to contain her urge to gag. They grabbed the footboard and struggled to shift the heavy bed. The wooden bedposts scratched against the hardwood with each spurt.

Adam stared down at the image etched into the floor. "Of course. Another pentagram. What the hell is going on with this house?"

Emma stepped into the pentagram's center. "If the book is so special, she would have kept it close. Not on a shelf, and not in plain sight."

"What are you doing?"

She rolled her foot back and forth on the hardwood, and the boards wobbled. "These boards have been cut." She knelt, hooked her finger in a small notch in the wood, and pried a board loose while Adam stared wide-eyed. Emma lowered her hand into the gap and immediately felt a hard object wrapped in velvet. She gripped it and pulled it out from under the floor. "No freaking way." She slowly unwrapped the object until its leather cover caught the overhead light. As Emma ran her hand along the light-tan cracked leather and flipped the book over, she noticed the distinct ridges of a face protruding from its cover. "This is it."

"It was my idea to move the bed." Adam grinned as he reached for the book.

Emma pulled her phone from her pocket. "Zero bars, of course. I'm going to go outside and try to call the Reverend. Remember what he said. Don't open it." She stepped through the balcony door and onto the rotting deck. She toggled her phone into airplane mode and back to cellular and watched with anticipation as a single bar, then two lit up on the top of her screen.

As Emma sat on the ledge of the balcony, she opened her phone's browser and plugged several search terms into the search engine. She tried *spirit books* first, but the phrase returned some obscure series about horses. She typed in several other phrases, but only when she searched for *historic demon books* did something useful pop up.

"Grimoire," she said under her breath.

The images slowly loaded on her phone screen, and as they trickled in, she saw pictures of books that looked eerily similar to the ones lining the shelves of the library, but none so intricate as the one they'd found under the floorboards.

"Books of magic containing instructions for the casting of spells, enchantment of objects, and conjuration of supernatural entities including demons," she read aloud. "This is real." Her thumb swiped on the smooth glass as she scrolled through her contact list and tapped the entry for the Reverend.

As she looked through the checkered glass at the streaky black stars lining the walls, the Reverend picked up. "Hello."

"Reverend?"

"Speaking."

"This is Emma. We found the book."

"The book," he said after a moment's pause.

"It's covered with a sculpted leather face and was buried under a satanic star. They're everywhere. We found them under the wallpaper and under the bed—"

"Where is the book now?" he asked.

"Adam's got it. I just went outside to make the call."

"I'll ring the driver, and we'll be over in ten minutes. Pack your bags."

"Thank you, Reverend."

"Have you seen Rosalie?"

Emma's thoughts flashed to the rotting face in the basement. "She's here, and she's not happy. But we're okay. She's keeping a low profile."

"Be careful. If she knows you're trying to leave with the book—well—just take care of yourself." The Reverend ended the call.

A gust of cold air sent a shiver up her spine, and she pushed herself to her feet and headed back inside. Although Adam had put the fire out, wood still hissed in the fireplace. She crossed the room, careful to avoid the pentagram, and knelt next to where he sat in the old armchair. "The Reverend is on his way."

He handed the book to Emma and rose to his feet. "Let's grab our bags and go. Forget the rest of our stuff."

As he approached the door, a primal shriek exploded off the walls, and the room felt as if it had been instantly depressurized, making Emma fall backward. The ceiling lamp swing violently overhead, casting off years' worth of dust, and its lights flickered and pulsed until the bulbs burst as another scream filled the room.

Emma, still disoriented, scrambled to her feet. "Are you all right?" She could barely hear herself over the ringing in her ears.

Adam had fallen against the doorframe and slowly raised his arm to point at the bed behind her. Emma turned to see the comforter rise from the center as the dried puddle of black goo appeared to rehydrate before her eyes.

As Adam pulled Emma up by her arm, the comforter fell away, revealing the skeletal form underneath. The old woman appeared to be deteriorating as she approached, blood and hunks of skin sloughing off her decaying form.

"Come on!" Adam's shouts sounded like whispers.

She tucked the book under her arm and scrambled toward the door. She looked back just in time to see the woman launch toward her with her yellowed hands outstretched. As Emma slammed the bedroom door shut, the woman hit it from the other side with so much force that the floor shook beneath their feet.

Another shriek echoed through the hallway as Emma's feet landed on the dusty second-floor carpet. A cold blast hit her back, and Emma glanced over her shoulder to see Rosalie breaking through the bedroom door.

The sound of carpeting being torn loose came from behind her. Again, Emma shot a look over her shoulder, this time just long enough to see a wave of the dusty floor covering barreling toward them. Adam reached the stair-case, but the bulging carpet caught up to Emma, and she tripped into a wooden wardrobe. As Rosalie closed in, Adam reached back frantically for his sister. Rosalie flicked her arm and tossed him against the closet door like a rag doll.

The ghoul hung close to Emma, drops of bloody pus plopping against her sneakers. The woman lowered herself, leaning forward and hovering over her like a rotting mirror image of herself. Emma lay frozen in fear and could do little more than shield herself from the putrid drips as Rosalie opened her mouth as if to speak.

"Give it to me!" Adam shouted from behind.

Emma snapped to and flung the book over her head toward her brother.

The woman's gaze shifted, and a guttural growl left her gaping maw, along with spurts of black spoiled rot, the smell of which made Emma want to vomit. "Go!" she shouted. Once the ghost had floated past, Emma flipped onto her stomach.

Adam reached the halfway point on the steps before the ghoul caught up to him. With another spectral swipe, she sent him tumbling over the wooden banister, and a sickening thud followed from the stone floor below.

CHAPTER TEN

Emma gave a panicked scream. Without thinking, she lunged toward the steps and slid stomach first under the ghost and down the carpeted staircase, crashing into the landing wall below. She scrambled to the stone floor and looked over to check on her brother.

The scene reminded her of her first visit to the house, with Adam sprawled on the ground and blood surrounding his head, only this time, he'd left real bits of himself on the stone. She crawled toward him and placed her hand on his chest as a sinking feeling worked its way through the pit of her stomach.

"Adam." Her voice cracked. "Please wake up. We've got to go."

The ghoul floated above her, hovering over the railing and moving into the center of the foyer.

"Adam!" She slapped him hard on the cheek.

His eyes cracked as she leaned over him.

"We've got to go. Can you move?" Her voice broke as panicked tears crept down her cheeks.

Adam's eyes rolled to the back of his head, then he snapped to as if waking from a terrible nightmare. He sat up and grabbed the back of his head. "What happened?" He pulled his hand away, and his fingers were wet with blood. "Where is she?" He looked up toward the ceiling and toward the specter staring down upon him. "Holy shit!"

Emma turned just in time to see Rosalie lunge and darted to the front door. She gripped the knob and twisted frantically, but the door refused to budge, and her hand tingled as if the house had been electrified. The window pulleys squealed to life as the single-pane windows in the dining room slid closed, shedding flakes of chipped paint as they ground against their aged wooden frames. The curtain tassels slithered loose from their knots as the heavy drapes fell slack and slunk along the floor, blocking the moon's glow and trapping her inside a house that now felt like a decrepit tomb.

I'm going to die here.

"Try the back!" Adam yelled as he pulled her toward the kitchen.

The ghoul splattered blood against the stone floor as she landed and hobbled toward them.

"I think we pissed her off!" he shouted as the house rumbled around them.

Headlights flashed through the front door, reflecting off the paneled glass and casting shards of white light on the foyer walls.

"The Reverend's here," Emma panted. Her eyes darted to the dining room table and the heavy wooden chairs underneath. "I'll distract her. Break a window."

Emma lifted the book up as the woman's eyes followed closely, her thick black pupils wide and surrounded by stale yellow and angry red veins. "Want this?"

Rosalie reached toward her with outstretched fingers twisting at unnatural angles.

"Break the damn window!" Emma shouted once more.

Adam rushed toward the end of the dining room table and pulled a chair from underneath.

Rosalie lurched toward Emma, her limbs snapping into place with each step.

Adam ripped the curtains aside and, with a great heave, launched the heavy wooden chair into the glass. The pane shattered in the center, sending a shower of glass to the floor as the top of the window came down in a single sharp sheet. "Come on!" He laid some of the curtain over the window to protect them from any jagged edges.

Rosalie's head snapped to the window as she let out a sickening growl. Emma lunged toward her brother, and he guided her over the ledge, her arm snagging on a piece of glass that hung from the side of the frame. She gritted her teeth as she tumbled onto the grass and turned to help her brother clear the window. Adam launched himself head-first and barrel-rolled onto the ground behind her. A shriek echoed through the house and burst through the window, carrying through the crisp night air.

"Are you okay?" he asked as he regained his footing. "You're bleeding."

"No time. Let's get to the gate." She couldn't bring herself to look at the gash but felt the warm blood trickling down her arm.

The Reverend's Cadillac straddled the open gate, but as Adam and Emma approached, the metal hinges squealed, and the gate slammed shut, trapping them inside the wrought-iron prison. The door of the house flew open, and an inhuman scream exploded from within.

The Reverend's face was gaunt in the moonlight as he stared back at the house. His eyes flashed to the two escapees. "I'm so glad you're okay."

Emma wrapped her fingers around the gate spindles and pulled frantically, but the heavy wrought iron refused to budge.

"Can you climb over?" the Reverend asked.

Emma looked up at the spikes that lined the top of the gate then back at the house.

"I'll boost you," Adam said.

Emma set the book on the ground and gripped the

bars, and Adam lifted her from behind. The iron fence was two times Emma's height, and even though Adam lifted her more than halfway, she had to rely on the full strength of her upper body to pull herself to the top and over the edge to the other side. The Reverend guided her to the ground, but Adam remained trapped on the other side.

"How do we get him over?" she asked.

Adam turned toward the house. "The ladder's on the side of the house, if I can just get to it."

"You can't go back there," she said.

"Keep this safe." He handed Emma the book. "I love you, and I'll be right back. Promise."

Emma tried to grab Adam through the gate, but he was already out of reach. She clenched the iron spindles that began to shake as Adam approached the house.

"Get in the car," the Reverend shouted over the clank of heavy metal. "I'll wait for him."

"I can't—" Emma's hands felt fused to the gate as Rosalie appeared on the front porch. Her gaze shifted to Adam, who froze in place midway across the front lawn.

Emma yanked with all her might on the gate, to no avail. "Hey!" She held the book through the spindles. "I've still got your book, you old bitch!"

Without another moment's hesitation, Adam darted toward the side of the house while the ghost locked eyes with Emma. A crash came from the side of the house, and

Adam let out a yelp that drew the woman's attention. She hovered over the front steps and drifted into the yard.

"No! Over here!" Emma shouted, her heart beating so hard it hurt.

As Rosalie disappeared around the corner, a green flash exploded through the yard, followed by Adam's agonized screaming. Emma's heart couldn't pump the blood fast enough, and her head went woozy. She backed against the car to steady herself as her legs began to wobble.

"Are you all right, dear?" The Reverend rushed toward her as her knees buckled. "I've got you." He gripped her waist tightly and eased her to the ground.

"Make sure Adam is okay," she slurred.

"I will. Don't you worry." The Reverend reached up and frantically knocked on the car window. "I need some help out here!"

The driver emerged from the front seat and helped to lift Emma into the back. "Are you all right, miss?"

Emma didn't respond, couldn't respond. Instead, she ran her fingers along the maroon velvet seat lining as her head spun. Her arm screamed with pain, which had been made ten times worse by the vault over the fence that had stretched her torn flesh. With her fleeting strength, she lifted her head and looked out into the front yard. A form appeared from around the corner of the house, lugging a wooden ladder.

"Look!" She pointed. "He made it!"

Adam scrambled across the yard, with Rosalie following close behind. He set the ladder underneath the gate and climbed to the top rung then put his feet on one of the gate's floral patterns and lifted himself over the top, careful to avoid the spikes.

As soon as Adam's feet hit the soil, he rushed to the back seat, where Emma tried to wrap her arms around him.

"Let's get back to the house," the Reverend said as Adam squeezed inside.

With a loud clink, the wrought-iron gate came loose and squealed open.

Adam lifted his middle finger high in the air and held it out to the woman, who now stood, helpless, at the gate, staring angrily at the car. "You lost!" He turned toward the Reverend. "She can't follow us, can she?"

The Reverend shook his head and pulled the door shut. "I hope not."

Emma's head fell limply against the back seat.

"Jesus." Adam leaned over her.

"I'm okay," she mumbled as the world spun around her. "Is she following us?"

Adam peered out the back window. "No, she's just standing behind the gate."

"Thank God."

"Is she bleeding badly?" the Reverend asked.

Emma winced as Adam rolled her arm over. "I don't

know. She's got a nasty cut, but it doesn't look like it's bleeding that badly."

"Just keep her arm above her heart. We'll be at the house in no time."

Adam leaned Emma against the window and wrapped her arm around his shoulder. "Just like car rides when we were little kids, huh?" He shook her head. "Remember the trip out West, when we played board games in the back of the station wagon the whole time?"

Emma grinned. "And you got carsick and threw up out the window."

"The poor guy behind us never saw it coming."

Emma felt warm droplets on her forehead as she rested her head on his shoulder.

The Reverend leaned over and pulled bottles of water from the minifridge under the bar.

Adam twisted off the plastic cap and held the bottle to Emma's lips. "Don't get used to this kind of treatment."

The cold water coated Emma's sandpaper tongue. She kept her head on Adam's shoulder as the car wound around the forest roads. As her head spun, she flashed back to her first journey to the house and let out a weak laugh. "This is the last time I work with you. Or at least, I'm picking the jobs from now on."

"Deal," he replied, "but after this, I'm sticking to desk jobs."

Emma's vision went in and out, and when she came to, Yvonne was leaning over her in the back seat.

"I think she's in shock," the Reverend said.

"What happened up there?" Yvonne asked. "Should we take her to the hospital?"

"They found the book," the Reverend replied. "Just get her inside."

Darkness crept from the corners of Emma's vision once more, and her head fell back on the headrest.

"Quickly," the Reverend snapped, his voice echoing through Emma's head as her thoughts went fuzzy and her world went black.

CHAPTER ELEVEN

S*leep. I just want to sleep.* Emma came to with a jolt, and Adam rushed toward her side.

"Take it easy." He tried to ease her back down into bed. Gauze wrapped the top of his head.

As everything came into focus, so did the events of the last few hours, or had it been days? "How long have I been out?"

"Just an hour or two."

She rolled her arm over and examined the blood-stained bandage.

"You cut yourself pretty deep," Adam said, "but it looks like you missed all the vital arteries. The Rev's wife stitched you up. She said it was probably the shock that got you, that you just needed a little rest."

"But what about your head? You could have a concussion. We should go to the hospital." Emma tried to sit up, but the blood rushed to her head.

"Just relax. Yvonne's going to give the hospital a call. If we need to go, we'll go, but it's a forty-five-minute drive."

Emma lay back down. "And we got the book, right?"

"The Reverend is taking care of it. There goes the rest of our ten grand, but I guess that's a small price to pay for saving the world."

"Saving the world?"

"That's what I'm telling myself," he replied. "Makes it easier to stomach."

Emma slowly scooted herself up against the headboard. The walls of the room were stark, white, and bare aside from a large piece of black-and-white abstract art, its straight lines and austere style mirroring the sleek environment. Adam rested his hand on the smooth metal frame of the bed's footboard. The leather chair in which he sat looked like something from the cover of a design magazine.

"Definitely a nice change from the old lady's house, isn't it?" he asked.

A soft knock at the door startled them. Yvonne entered and smiled when she saw Emma sitting up in bed. "So glad to see you're awake."

"I'm feeling a lot better," Emma replied. "Still light-headed, but better."

"That'll go away with rest and a decent meal." Yvonne sat on the bed. "You two have had quite the night."

Adam chuckled. "That's an understatement."

"Miss," a voice said through the crack in the door. "Dinner's almost ready."

Emma looked at her phone. "It's almost midnight. A little late for dinner, isn't it?"

Yvonne sat up straighter on the bed. "You must get your strength back."

"That's very kind of you. Thank you," Emma replied.

"Go wash up, and we'll meet you in the dining room. I left a fresh set of clothes and a towel for you in the restroom. Figured you'd like to change and shower before dinner. I took a guess at your size."

Emma looked down at her blood-soaked clothing. Fortunately, someone had placed a pad underneath her to keep the blood and grime off the fresh sheets.

Yvonne gestured for Adam to follow. "Let's leave your sister so she can freshen up."

Emma slid her legs over the edge of the bed. Her head swam at first, and she closed her eyes and took several deep breaths until the spinning stopped. Her arm ached as she used it to push herself off the bed. She took a few cautious steps toward the leather chair and leaned against it to steady herself.

The bathroom's chilly black and white ceramic tiles reminded her of Rosalie's. Her dirty clothing fell to the floor as she stripped down to nothing but the bandage holding her arm together. A white sundress hung from the back of the door, and a pair of boy shorts sat on the counter with white flats perched next to them. Yvonne had also left a fresh bandage next to a tube of antibiotic ointment.

I would kill for a pair of yoga pants. Emma reached into the walk-in shower and turned the knob. Water cascaded from the square showerhead, and she waited with anticipation for the water to warm.

The bandage. She cringed at the thought of removing it but doubted the thing would survive the shower. The adhesive pulled her hair and clung to her skin as she carefully tugged it away. *Don't look,* she told herself, but as the bandage pulled free, she couldn't resist the temptation. For all the blood, the gash itself was only an inch long, and Yvonne had stitched the loose flaps of skin together with neat black crisscrosses.

As steam clung to the glass of the shower, she stepped inside, careful not to get her arm wet until she was prepared for the inevitable sting. The water hit her body, and she watched bloody brown streaks trickle down her legs and into the shower drain as she washed the filth of the house from her body—as she washed Rosalie from her body.

She drew the wound under the water for a moment, just long enough to wash the dried blood away. *Am I even supposed to get this wet?*

Emma could have lived in the shower until her skin pruned and the water ran cold. She counted down from five and forced herself to shut off the faucet. Steam lingered as she opened the shower door, pulled the towel in quickly from the rack next to her, and shut the door once more to prevent the chill from rushing in. She toweled herself off then stepped onto the cold tile floor. After rubbing a coat of antibiotic ointment on her wound, she stuck the fresh bandage over it and put on the clothes Yvonne had left for her.

The hardwood floor in the hallway didn't creak as it had in the old house, but Emma still walked as if ghosts waited in the wings. Conversation trailed in from the dining room, but when she reached the entryway, those sitting at the table stopped talking and stared at her. Adam sat at the center, with the Reverend and his wife at opposite ends.

The smell of pan-seared meat hit Emma's nose and blended with the scents of grime and rot that still lingered in her nostrils. Her stomach gurgled, and she swallowed hard to squelch the nausea. "I'm not feeling well. I may go back to the room and lie down."

"Oh, nonsense," Yvonne said. "You need to eat something to keep your strength up."

"I'm not hungry."

"Please, dear, just come sit with us. Even if you just pick a little, you've got to eat. We could at least make you a cup of coffee."

Emma sighed. "Okay, maybe just a cup."

"How are you feeling?" Adam asked as she sat across from him.

"Better." She looked at the Reverend. "Thanks again for everything."

The cook entered a few moments later with a cup of piping-hot coffee before setting plates for the other three. Yvonne sipped her red wine while the Reverend made small talk. Adam sliced through his steak and gulped from his wineglass, enjoying another unexpected brush with luxury as Emma slowly drank her coffee.

Yvonne cast a casual glance at Emma. "So, you and your brother come from New York?"

"We both grew up there," Emma answered on autopilot while her brain tried to make sense of the events of the past week. "You never told us much about yourself last time. Do you work for the church too?"

Yvonne smiled at the Reverend from across the table. "If you'd told me I'd grow up to be a reverend's wife, I wouldn't have believed you, but now I couldn't imagine doing anything else." She leaned in. "You have to tell us what happened tonight. What was it like up there?"

Images of Rosalie flashed through Emma's mind. "Hell."

Yvonne smirked. "Where did you find the book?"

Emma's stomach burbled once more. "She had hidden it underneath her bed, under the floorboards. I just can't make any sense of it. It's like she was protecting it."

The Reverend brushed his wife's arm. "Let's quit with the interrogation for now. Our guests have been through enough for one evening."

Adam dropped his knife on the floor. "God dammit," he said under his breath before realizing his audience. "Sorry." He leaned over to grab his lost piece of silverware.

The Reverend stared intently. "Everything all right?"

"Fine, just a little tired is all." Adam returned to his meal and slid his knife across the plate as he attempted to cut his steak. The knife dug into the ceramic.

Emma winced. "Would you watch what you're doing?"

Adam looked down at his plate as his eyes widened. "Sorry. I don't know what's wrong with me." He tried once more with the knife, but it fell free from his hand and crashed into the plate. He held his hand in front of him and wiggled his fingers. "I can't—something's wrong." He tried to stand, but his legs buckled as he fell forward and pulled his plate with him to the floor.

"Adam!" Emma rushed to the other side of the table and knelt next to him. "Are you all right?" She rolled him over onto his back.

"Too much wine, perhaps," the Reverend said.

As Emma stood, blood rushed to her head, and she caught herself on the back of Adam's chair.

The Reverend clasped his hands. "You two must be very tired."

"Help me," she pled, but neither the Reverend nor Yvonne moved from the table.

Emma's legs wobbled underneath her, and she fell into the chair, bouncing against her tailbone. "I don't feel well." She massaged her temples and shut her eyes.

"Maybe you should lie down with your brother," Yvonne replied.

"What are you talking about?" Emma grabbed the stem of Adam's empty wineglass and noticed a small pinch of white powder that had settled at the bottom. "What did you put in our drinks?"

Yvonne shot the Reverend a glance. "You've had a stressful day. We just gave you both a little something to take the edge off and help you sleep for a few hours."

The Reverend chuckled. "You two are very important, you know. It took us years to track down that book, and we're very grateful you've brought it to us."

Emma pushed herself up off the chair but tripped over her feet and stumbled to the floor.

"Careful." Yvonne approached. "You don't want to hurt yourself before the big ceremony tomorrow night." She knelt next to Emma as Adam let out a soft groan. "We'll need your help to make it a success." The room swirled as Yvonne leaned over her. "We've got big plans for you."

The woman's skin seemed to bubble as Emma's vision

spun. Emma laid her head back on the ground, and despite her best efforts to stay awake, the world faded to darkness.

"Call the others," the Reverend said just as everything went dark.

CHAPTER TWELVE

E mma awoke in the dark bedroom with a pounding headache. Her hands had been bound behind her with rope woven through the chair slats, and the scratchy fibers dug into her wrists and refused to give. The lingering haze from the drugs faded, and a sickening realization settled in. *People who tie you up never let you go.*

The alarm clock next to the bed cast a faint red glow. She'd only slept for an hour. Whatever drugs Yvonne had given her must have worn off too early. She thought back to Adam's empty wineglass. He'd drunk it all, but she'd only taken a few sips of coffee. She looked down at the rope binding her legs to the chair. The Reverend and Yvonne must have counted on her sleeping for a few more hours, because they hadn't bothered to bind her with much care. If she could tip over the chair without causing too much noise, she might be able to slip the ropes binding her legs free from underneath it.

The bed she'd slept in earlier sat a few feet away and could pad her fall if she could just scoot close enough. She jostled her body sideways, and the legs of the chair whined against the floor as it slid an inch closer toward the bed. She listened for a reaction, but the dim drone of conversation in the dining room carried on. The area rug scrunched against the chair legs as Emma edged closer to the bed. She twisted round until her back was turned to the mattress, held her breath, and pushed off against the floor.

Her world went sideways as the chair back bounced against the mattress. But instead of coming to rest, the back legs screeched against the hardwood and slid out from under her, falling to the floor with a loud *thunk* and mashing her hands between the chair slats and the floor.

Emma let out a pained cry and slid the rope free from under the chair legs as the chatter outside stopped and footsteps approached. In a panic, she brought her feet up to the chair seat and pressed against it, pulling the ropes around her wrist as hard as she could manage. Pain shot through her arms as she wrenched against the rope and compressed her throbbing fingers until her hands slid free.

The door slammed open, and light flooded the room. Yvonne stood in the doorway, and a man clad in all black pushed her aside. Without thinking, Emma picked up the chair and rammed it into his chest as hard as she could, forcing them both back outside the doorway. She dropped the chair, slammed the door, and clicked the latch into place.

Emma ripped the curtains aside and unlatched the window. The door cracked behind her as someone slammed against it, but she had no time to look back. She lifted one leg over the ledge, then the other, and launched herself off the side of the house and onto the grass below.

Shouts came from the bedroom as she scrambled to her feet.

A sobering realization settled in as Emma debated her choices. She could try to make it to the main road and follow it to town, but that would leave her exposed, and odds were she wouldn't make it far without being captured. Even if she made it, she had no idea what awaited her when she arrived. The alternative put a knot in her stomach. If she could get back to the house, she could take the car. But that meant she'd have to go back inside for the keys.

The front door of the Reverend's house slammed open. Emma scrambled into the woods, the tangles of limbs and uneven rocks slowing her pace. The moonlight flashed through the trees as she sprinted toward the house on the hill. Branches snapped behind her as voices obscured the forest soundtrack. She pushed harder, determined to get to the house, and her chest tightened as she struggled to catch her breath.

Thoughts of Adam raced through her head. *What have they done to him? Is he still alive?* But she pushed those questions to the back of her mind, determined to focus on the task at hand. She wouldn't do either of them any good captured.

Her lungs burned with each breath, and just as she'd started to contemplate surrender, she stumbled into the stream bordering the road to Rosalie's house. She splashed through the shin-deep water and climbed the short drop-off to the road.

She must have run a mile by the time she reached the wrought-iron gates as shouts echoed in the distance. "No, why's it closed?" she panted as she reached for a spindle and pushed. The gate held firm. "No, no, no!" Tears crept from the corners of her eyes as she pulled frantically.

A car engine roared in the distance, and Emma turned to see headlights flashing through the breaks in the trees.

"They're coming for me." Emma's heart rate quickened, and she looked at the top of the gate. "There's no way I can climb that." She turned back to see the headlights growing closer.

Out of options, she faced the house and screamed. "They're going to kill me!" Her voice strained against the wind. "I didn't know about the book! I'm sorry!"

As the car approached, she backed against the gate. Headlights broke over the hill, blinding her in a sudden flash. She held onto the spindles as if they were life preservers. "I will help you get the book back!" she screamed.

At first, she thought the car might slam into her, crushing her against the gate, but then Emma felt the gate shift, leaving just enough room for her to slip through to the other side. The gate slammed shut behind her as she ran toward the house—toward the very thing from which she'd fled in terror hours before. She reached for the front doorknob and twisted. The foyer was dark, and although the weather outside was cool, the inside of the house was so cold it caused instant goose bumps. She spotted her car keys on the dining room table and tried to catch her breath as she stared out the front window. The car on the other side of the gate sat idle but blocked her only path of escape.

The chill followed her into the living room, and she wondered how long she could safely move through the house without confronting its resident ghost. But surely, Rosalie had heard her promise—it was the only reason why Emma wasn't pancaked against that front gate. Her breath spiraled in front of her. "It's fucking freezing."

The living room fireplace erupted in flame, and logs crackled and hissed as they caught. Emma checked her surroundings as switches popped around her and the lights throughout the house turned on. A part of her wanted to run, but the warmth of the fire was too inviting to flee. She spotted Adam's cellphone on the end table next to the couch. Although the Reverend's wife must have taken Emma's, in all the commotion, Adam had left his behind.

At first, she thought to dial 911. But she had no idea what the Reverend and his wife were going to do or how far his grip reached. She picked up Adam's phone and flicked through the list of contacts. "Book Jerkoff," she said under her breath. The thought of calling the man sent a shiver up her spine. If he wanted the book badly enough, maybe he'd be willing to help. She didn't have much to lose.

But she needed a signal. Emma swallowed hard to squelch a wave of nausea and dashed toward the stairs. Light from the wall sconces cast eerie shadows along the wall as Emma reached the staircase to the third floor. The doors sat open, and firelight from Rosalie's bedroom flickered down the narrow hallway.

As soon as Emma reached Rosalie's balcony, she tapped the contact. "Come on, you son of a bitch." She held her breath and waited for ringing on the other end. After a few moments of silence, the call went through.

"Hello," said the voice on the other end.

"It's all gone wrong. The Reverend—he has the book. They've taken my brother." She'd been so concerned with getting through to someone that she hadn't bothered to form a coherent sentence.

The person on the other end stayed silent for what felt like minutes, and if it hadn't been for the faint breathing coming through the receiver, she would have assumed the call had disconnected. "Where are you?" His voice was gravelly as if shredded by years of cigars and early-afternoon scotches.

"I made it back to the house."

"Stay where you are, and I'll send someone."

"I can't leave my brother."

"If you leave the house, they will kill you. Now, stay put while I figure out how to unbungle the mess you've made."

"The mess we've made?" Emma asked. "Why didn't you tell us about what we were getting ourselves into? Why didn't you tell us about the Reverend?" She gripped the phone so hard she probably would have broken it had she gripped much harder.

"If I had, would your brother have agreed to the job?" The receiver clicked.

"God dammit!" Emma would have thrown the phone had it not been her only lifeline to the outside world.

Several other cars had gathered outside during her brief call. Emma assumed it was only a matter of time before they either climbed the fence or rammed through it. But the longer she stood, the more she wondered why they hadn't made a move.

Static cling sent a shiver up her arm. She could feel the same presence as she had before, watching the landscape with her. But although Emma felt safe for the moment, so

much of the situation sat just beyond her realm of compre-
hension. *Why the pentagrams? Why the demonic artifacts?*
She stood in front of the window for what felt like
hours. Eventually, two of the three cars pulled away,
leaving only one behind to stand guard.

"Do I just sit here and wait? I should do something."
She searched the room for a weapon with which to defend
herself and settled on a fire poker. If they were to come for
her, she would die before she let them take her. She'd claw
their eyes out with her fingernails if she had to.

She pushed the armchair closer to the fireplace, took a
seat, and let the heat wash over her. She would have done
anything to escape the creepy estate before, but now she
clung to it like a security blanket. She felt the woman in
the walls and in the surrounding air, and the two seemed to
have a mutual understanding. *Keep me safe, and I'll get
your book back.* Emma had no clue how she'd deliver on
her end of the bargain, but she would try.

She pulled a blanket from a hall closet and sat in front
of the fireplace, but no matter how close she drew the chair
toward it, the chill of loneliness persisted. She walked
toward the window now and then to check the front yard.
The black car remained, headlights off but still there all the
same. Whoever waited for her on the other side of the gate
would ensure that she never left.

Sleep came but with paranoid dreams truncated
every half hour by sudden jolts and cold sweats. The

sound of breathing woke her. She kept her eyes closed at first, hoping it was all part of a dream, and attempted to call back the fleeting sleep that had finally given her a moment's rest. She wiped the crust from her eyes as the firelight came into focus. The frizzy-haired woman in white hovered in front of the fireplace, and the crackling flame cut through her as if she were made of thin fabric. Emma's first instinct was to cry out or scream, but she swallowed the urge and instead silently scooted up in her chair to dull the ache in her back.

The woman floated in front of the family photo sitting on the mantel.

"Is that you in the picture?" Emma's voice came out squeaky and timid.

The woman turned toward Emma. Her face was gaunt, with deep bags underneath her sunken eyes, but she wasn't the terrifying creature Emma had met earlier. As she drew closer, Emma recognized the pencil-thin nose, high cheekbones, and weak chin from the picture in her bedroom.

"Rosalie's a pretty name."

The woman's eyes widened as if it had been the first time someone had said her name in decades.

Emma searched for the right question to ask. "Why do you want the book?"

Rosalie leaned in and reached for Emma's hand that

rested on the arm of the chair. Her voice was barely more than a raspy whisper. "To protect."

"To protect the book?"

"The world."

Emma rubbed her chin. "From those who'd use the book to hurt others. You wanted to keep it locked away."

Rosalie nodded.

The weight of her burden must have been heavy, protecting the book for decades from an evil force that lingered in the shadows. Emma noticed sparkly drips coming from the woman's eyes, like tears of glitter trickling to the floor. Guilt washed over her as she thought of how the woman had wasted away in that house, fulfilling her duty, and Emma had ruined it.

All she could think to say was "For what it's worth, I'm sorry." The words came with a fresh set of tears. "I've called for help, and I'll do everything I can to get your book back. The man on the phone—he sent my brother here to find the book and is sending help now. Can I trust him?"

Rosalie's lips curled into the slightest smile as she reached for Emma's face. As her cool palm left condensation on Emma's cheek, a strange feeling rose in Emma's chest—peace. The feeling had been fleeting in Emma's life.

As Rosalie lifted her hand away and drifted once more toward the fireplace, Emma returned her smile. The past was out of her control, and her mind settled on a singular absolute truth. *I will make this right.*

CHAPTER THIRTEEN

Dawn came and went, but Emma remained plastered to the chair in the third-floor bedroom, waiting for what, she didn't know. A knock at the front door pulled her from a daydream. At first, she thought she'd imagined it, and she waited with bated breath until a pounding came a few minutes later.

She crossed the room to the checkered window and looked down into the yard below. Two forms lay splayed on either side of the black car parked outside the gate, and a yellow convertible was stationed at the base of the front steps.

Emma crept down the stairs and through the foyer, clutching the metal fire poker. She had no good way to tell who waited on the other side of the door without giving herself away, so she poked her head around the corner and tried to glimpse the intruder through the paneled door glass.

"Would you open the damned door?" a woman shouted from the other side. "I can see you in there. If I'd wanted to kill you, you'd be dead already."

"What do you think, Rosalie? Should I let her in?" Emma asked.

The knob on the front door lock twisted, and the door creaked open.

"Guess that's a yes," Emma said under her breath.

The woman stood a few inches shorter than Emma, hardly an imposing figure. She glanced casually through the doorway. "About time." She pushed past Emma and into the foyer.

"Who are you?" Emma's hand was still wrapped so tightly around the poker her knuckles had gone white.

The woman pulled a leather bag from her back and flung it onto the dining room table. She wore a green vest with a linen blouse tucked into a pair of crimson pants leading to bulky leather boots. Her black shoulder-length hair bobbed as she turned toward Emma. "Marie." She said the name as if it provided some explanation.

"But who are you?" Emma asked again.

Marie rolled her eyes. "You should know. You're the one who called. They sent me for the book."

Emma shrugged.

"I'm a fixer. I've come to rectify a criminal level of

incompetence, one that may threaten everything you know and love—the entire world, really." She put her hands on her hips. "And I'm not sure what you're planning to do with that metal stick, but I'd feel better if you put it down."

"What about the man on the phone?" Emma set the poker on the dining room table.

Marie scowled. "He'll be lucky if he can get a job flipping burgers after this, if all the burger joints aren't destroyed in a fiery apocalypse." She unzipped her leather bag. "Leave it to a man to pay punks to do his dirty work. Had he come here himself to reclaim the book, we wouldn't be in this situation. Although I'm sure he'd have figured out some way to screw that up too."

Emma's head swam with questions, but Marie kept talking as if Emma completely understood the situation. "Will you tell me what the hell is going on? My brother's been taken by some crazy cult, and if I'm not mistaken, you've just murdered two people outside."

Marie shook her head. "Your brother was tasked with the job of retrieving a grimoire containing the name of one of existence's most powerful demons. The cult you're referring to has tracked it for some time, and a few years ago, they figured out that it was located in this very house."

Emma's mouth hung agape.

"And that book could mean terrible things for all of us —for humanity itself. So I'm here to get it back."

"Why haven't they come for me? I'm a sitting duck in this house."

Marie paused. Then she approached a dining room window. "You see those markings on the front of the gate out there?"

"Yeah."

"They're Marian symbols. The eye, the *V*s—they're scattered all around the house."

"But what do they do?"

"They protect the book and the inhabitants of the house from common outside evils, including followers of the left-hand path and lesser demons."

A chill ran up Emma's spine. *Demons?* She thought back to her encounters with the Reverend. He had never crossed the gate.

"But what about the pentagrams we found in her room and under her bed? They're signs of the devil."

Marie pulled a notebook from her bag and opened it to a blank page. She drew the five-pointed star in red ink then circled it. "This, you mean?"

"That's it."

She rolled her eyes. "You can thank pop culture for bastardizing that one. It's another protective symbol—a barrier between those who stand within it and the demons who'd threaten them. If it was under her bed, it was for protection."

"What about the shoes in the fireplace?"

Marie looked up from her notebook. "That's another outdated way of protecting the home. Shoes were believed to have confused evil spirits. They attack the shoes, thinking there are people attached to them, then get trapped inside."

"But this is all so—"

"Crazy?" Marie asked.

Emma nodded.

"No." Marie slammed her notebook shut. "What's crazy is that the family who's lived in this house has protected that book for centuries. What's crazy is that the watcher of this house was too goddamned lazy or scared to come here himself and sent two bumbling idiots who've delivered the book directly to the one group who'd do the most harm with it." She shot a spiteful glance at Emma.

"Bumbling idiots?" Emma's hand was starting to shake. "How were we supposed to know? No one bothered to tell us any of this."

Marie rubbed her forehead. "You're right. And I guess none of that matters now."

"What are we going to do? How are we going to fix this and save my brother?" Emma asked.

Marie laughed as she pulled a set of books from her bag. "Your brother is the least of my concerns. I'm here for the book, and that's it. You'll stay here while I go clean up the mess, and if you're lucky, we'll both make it out of this alive."

"I'm not leaving my brother to die," Emma replied. "I'm coming with you."

Marie pulled a leather wrap from her bag and unrolled it to reveal a line of shiny metal daggers. "Just be thankful you've survived this long. The charms and symbols should protect you while you're in the house, but if you leave, I guarantee you'll be dead by the next sunrise. You're a fool if you think you're equipped to help me."

"Then I'm a fool, and I'll die a fool." Hot tears streamed down her cheeks. "But I'm not leaving my brother behind."

"Fine." Marie waved her hand dismissively. "You can tag along. But if you get in my way, know that my one goal remains, and if that means pushing you into the fire, I'll do it with a smile. Humanity is more important than you or your brother."

Emma wiped her cheek and wondered how things could have become such a catastrophic mess. She swallowed hard and clenched her fist. "What's your plan?"

"If they're smart, the book's hidden away somewhere we'd never find it. But at some point, they'll want to use it."

Emma's eyes widened. "For a ceremony? Last night the Reverend mentioned that Adam and I were an important part of tonight's ceremony. It has to be tonight."

"Black Mass," Marie said. "Looks like tonight's the night, then."

"How do we stop them?"

Marie handed a dagger to Emma. "We slit their throats and take the book before they read the name inside."

"But we're probably talking about a few hundred people." Emma put her hands to her lips. "I just don't get it. The Reverend's just been sitting around and waiting for a chance to take the book?"

"That's right. Books like this are hidden all over the world. Houses like this one have served as vaults for generations, run by families who keep the books safe and ensure that they never leave the grounds. It's a bit of an outdated system, and because of other events like this, we're slowly merging books into protected libraries."

"You mean, things like this have happened before? How haven't they made the news?"

"They have," Marie replied, "just not in ways you might recognize. You've heard of the Mothman bridge?"

Emma nodded.

"That was small-scale."

"What about large-scale?"

Marie scanned the items scattered across the table as if deciding whether to answer. "In China a few years ago, two hundred people died by the time we contained it. You might have heard about a fertilizer-plant explosion—well, the Chinese government is good at covering things up."

Emma pulled up a chair at the dining room table and put her head in her hands.

"A lot to take in, isn't it?" Marie replied.

"We didn't know. The woman—Rosalie—nearly killed Adam. We didn't realize she was trying to protect the book."

"Unfinished business," Marie said. "You protect something for generations, and sometimes it's hard to let go of, even in death."

Emma scanned the minuscule collection of daggers on the table. "Do you know the scale of what's going on up the road?"

"What do you mean?"

"The Reverend's got a large congregation. How are a few daggers going to compete with hundreds, if not thousands, of people?"

"I'm very good at what I do," Marie replied. "Three book extractions and one doomsday scenario. And never underestimate the power of surprise."

"So, you've done this before?"

"This is different. *This* book should have been moved ages ago. We call it a tier one book, as in the creatures it's capable of unleashing aren't low-rung demons that'll throw dishes around the room."

"What's in the book, then?"

Marie rubbed her chin. "Think of it like this—mice will ruin your crops for the year, and lions will eat you alive. We're dealing with a lion."

"A lion—great."

Marie pulled a book from the stack on the table and

ventured to the couch in the living room.

"What are you doing?" Emma asked, following close on her heels.

"Research," Marie replied.

"Shouldn't we be doing something—sneaking in, girding our loins?" She clenched her fists so tight she left fingernail indents on her palm.

Marie looked up at her. "If we go now, we'll never be able to get to the book. We'll wait until they bring it out into the open. From the sound of it, with several hundred people and all, the ceremony tonight should be easy to spot."

"But they might kill him before—"

"They won't kill him. They'll need him for the ceremony." Marie's nonchalance gave Emma anxiety. After a few minutes of Emma pacing in front of the fireplace, Marie looked up once more from her book. "You're making it impossible to concentrate. Would you go somewhere else?"

Emma froze. "No. No I won't go somewhere else." She plopped down onto the couch next to Marie. "I know this is partially my fault."

"Understatement of the millennium."

Emma shook her head. "I get it. And I know I'm a nuisance." Marie continued reading but smirked. "But I can help you. I understand—if I get in the way, I'm axed. I don't care. But you can't deny that two are better than one.

I just need for you to show me how to help and give me a chance."

Marie's eyes darted from the text to Emma then back to the text. "I work best alone."

Emma looked down at the table. "Fine—I'll figure things out on my—"

"I wasn't finished," Marie said. "From what I've gathered, this grimoire housed the name of a demon of immense power."

"Who, Satan himself?"

Marie laughed. "Hardly. The dark lord has no reason to visit this place. But his general may."

"Satan has a general?"

"Several, and bringing a single one to Earth could be cataclysmic."

"So all the Reverend has to do is read a name in a book?"

"Not just a name. Each true name comes with a ritual. Complete the ritual, say the name in the book, and show the demon you're serious, and—well—unleash havoc."

"How do we stop it if the Reverend conjures one?"

Marie averted her eyes. "Let's just hope that doesn't happen. If a demon is conjured by name, it can be sent back with the same name, but that name could be pages long. You'd have to gain possession of the book to even get it right."

"And what about the ritual?"

"I can't say for sure. The lesser demons might take an offering or an animal sacrifice. But the higher-ups prefer humans."

Emma's heart sank. "That's what you meant about them needing Adam."

"So, if you want to be of help to me, you'll help me figure out where they plan to hold the ritual."

Emma perked up. "The Reverend said they'd been building a brand-new sanctuary in the industrial complex on the other side of the corn fields. If they're planning some massive ritual, it would have to be there."

"You've seen this place?"

Emma looked down at her lap. "Just from a distance."

"Think you could get us back there?"

"Yeah, it's easy to spot from the main road."

"Let's hope so." Marie stood from the chair.

"Are we leaving now?" Emma's stomach knotted. "When will the ceremony start?"

"When the full moon reaches its highest point. Probably a little before midnight, when the path between heaven and hell is clearest."

Emma followed her as she crossed to the front door and stepped outside. "Where are you going?"

Marie scanned the perimeter. "Let's assume there are a few hundred people, as you say. How would they know who to let in? Watch my back."

Aside from a few bodies at the front gates, the scene

outside was peaceful. Trees swayed in the autumn breeze, and a pair of squirrels circled around the wrought-iron spindles at the top of the perimeter wall. "Looks clear to me," Emma said.

Marie's boots kicked up dust as she pounded them into the gravel drive on her way to the gate. "You keep watching my back."

Emma lingered behind the gate's threshold. "Where are you going? It's not safe out there." She checked the tree line, but no one else had bothered to come. *What would be the point? They have what they wanted.* She grimaced when she looked at the men on the ground. Pools of oxidized blood had been absorbed by the dirt and formed dingy halos of reddish brown around the men's heads.

Marie flipped one man over and reached inside his jacket pocket. A gash on his neck was caked with dirt and dried blood. She pulled a card from his inside pocket. The small rectangle caught the sunlight, and its black metal surface shimmered. A symbol was etched in red—a double cross perched atop an infinity loop.

"What does it mean?" Emma asked.

"The Leviathan Cross." Marie walked to the other body sprawled in the dirt and fished out another card. She looked down upon the bald thug with a grizzled face who looked as if he'd taken right hooks daily. "Thankfully, these aren't picture IDs. Here." She flicked a card through the air toward Emma, who fumbled it. The card plinked as it hit the ground.

"Think we'll be able to get in with these?" Emma asked.

"That, or they'll kill us at the gates. But I've seen cards like this at high-profile ceremonies. I'm guessing we're talking about more than just a few hundred people."

Emma's mouth hung open as she ran her fingers along the Leviathan Cross then turned it over to examine the other side. She could feel tiny grooves covering it as if an intricate symbol had been carved on the other side as well. She held it up and let the sun hit its surface but was still unable to make out the shape.

Marie tugged one of the dead brutes toward the gate. "Want to see why no one would cross onto the grounds? Give me a hand with him."

Emma stepped through the gate and grabbed the man's free arm. Together, she and Marie tugged the body over the property's threshold. At first, the body lay dormant, but as they stood in the protection of the grand house, the man's fingers twitched. The motion became more violent, and his body moved as if he were submerged in boiling water. His skin changed, too, its pallor shifting from pale to deep red. The man's skin blistered and bubbled as his clothing deteriorated and fell into nothing.

Emma turned her head as his skin began to slough off. "Okay, I get it."

"You're missing the best part," Marie said. "And we need to dispose of both the bodies. We can't just leave them lying around for someone to find."

Emma waited until the sizzling stopped then helped Marie with the other body. She tried not to look, but after the gruesome sound had stopped once more, she took a quick look at the ground. Nothing remained except for two piles of ash and scorched grass.

Marie knelt and ran her hand over a splotch of green grass in the unkempt front yard. "We stand on blessed earth. Followers of the left-hand path can't cross. Houses like these have a whole slew of protections. Some of them we now know are bogus—crystals, for one—but others work against spirits and lesser demons at least."

"What about greater demons?"

Marie chuckled. "Like a shock collar to a dog, but some dogs are more determined than others."

CHAPTER FOURTEEN

The sun slipped behind the horizon, taking with it daylight's protection. Marie ran the edge of a dagger along a sharpening block at the dining room table. "We should leave soon."

Emma looked out the window. The moon hung crooked, halfway hidden behind the tree line, like a sharp sickle cutting into a darkening sky. "The moon's only a sliver tonight. Thought you said it would be full."

"The devil's light will fill it up." Marie slid the sharpened dagger into her boot then moved on to the next. She shot a look at Emma from the corner of her eye. "Find something black to wear."

Emma looked down at her ruby-red hoodie. "I'm not exactly wearing camouflage, I guess." She left Marie to sharpen and went to her bedroom, where she grabbed a pair of black jeans and a long-sleeved shirt. She caught a glimpse of herself in the mirror. Her face had fear written across it, complemented by her pale skin and tired eyes. She was sure the Reverend and his wife would recognize her from a mile away. She pulled her hair into a messy bun and grabbed a cap from her bag. "That's better," she said under her breath. She took several deep breaths until she was satisfied with the woman standing in the mirror. "You can do this. Do it for Adam."

"We'll take the car by the gate," Marie said as Emma entered the dining room. "We should blend right in."

"What if they recognize it?" Emma asked.

"It's a black car. I'm sure there will be others if we're talking about hundreds of people. We can ditch it in a field and walk the rest of the way if need be, and it'll be way less noticeable than a bright-yellow convertible. Maybe we can find a weak spot in a fence and blend in once we're inside. Just depends on how many people we're dealing with. But with the ID cards, we should be able to drive right through."

Emma leaned against the table. "And are we just supposed to waltz down the aisle and take the book in the middle of a satanic ceremony?"

Marie nodded. "That's exactly what we'll do. I'll strike before the Reverend knows what hit him then sneak out in the commotion. Once we're back at the house, we can grab the cars, and I'll take the book for final deposit."

Emma's mouth hung open as she chose her next words

carefully. "Look, I assume you know what you're doing, but this sounds like suicide to me."

"You're right, I do know what I'm doing. So either trust me or stay out of my way. The choice is yours."

"Thanks for the reassurance."

The crescent moon had cleared the trees and sat midway in the sky as they left the house for the industrial compound. Emma looked over her shoulder on the walk to the car, wondering if this would be the last time she'd set eyes on the place. Rosalie hovered behind the third-floor window. The woman had been the book's protector for so long, and now it was up to Emma to bring it back safely. She turned and gave a meek wave to the ghost who'd once tormented her. Rosalie pressed a hand against the checkered glass.

After they slipped through the gate, Marie reached for the handle of the driver's-side door, and Emma slid into the leather passenger's seat. Marie turned the keys, which still hung from the ignition. The boat of a car swayed, threatening to plow its bumper into the trees, before Marie managed to align it with the road and put it in drive. The house disappeared behind the hill in the rearview mirror as she pulled away, and the woman in the window still watched and waited until Emma could no longer see.

As the car twisted and turned down the road, tree limbs occasionally scraping its sides, Emma's stomach twisted as well at the thought of the task ahead. "Where are you from?" she asked after the silence had become too much to bear.

Marie scrunched her brow. "Nowhere."

"No, I mean, where did you grow up? Like, where were you born?"

Marie tightened her grip on the wheel. "Technically Wisconsin, but I've lived in Ohio, Pennsylvania, Massachusetts, Vermont, and New York. I guess I slowly worked my way up the East Coast."

"Your parents moved around a lot, then?"

Marie chuckled. "I moved around a lot, first with relatives, then with foster care. My mom died when I was born, and I guess my dad had better things to do than raise a kid."

"Oh, I'm sorry," Emma replied, slightly horrified by the emotional can of worms she'd opened.

"Don't be," Marie snapped. "I don't need your pity."

Emma shrank into her leather seat.

Marie glanced at her out of the corner of her eye, and her expression softened. "I'm sorry. It was a shitty childhood, but things worked out for the best."

"Are you a witch?" The question had lingered in Emma's mind for some time.

"You mean, do I put on a funny hat and fly around on a broomstick? Not quite."

"That's not what I—"

Marie laughed. "I know what you mean. No, I'm not a witch in the strictest sense of the term. I'm trained to use magical artifacts, but the blood running through my veins is the same as yours and the same as Rosalie's."

As Marie pulled toward the clearing beyond the woods, Emma spotted a row of taillights through the trees ahead. Cars lined the two-lane back road, stretching toward the highway in the distance. "Tonight's definitely the night," Emma said as they waited for a break in the traffic. "He's letting you out." She pointed toward the car that had stopped short of the intersection and a man who was waving them on. "They look just like ordinary people. What would make them want to be a part of something so evil?"

"Eternal reward. Take the left-hand path and live forever at His side, thriving on the backs of nonbelievers," Marie said casually as if reading from an informational pamphlet.

Emma shuddered. "I just can't imagine wanting to see others suffer in exchange for a personal reward."

"People do it every day. They lead lives of prescribed virtue while tormenting those who take their own paths. These people just do it in the name of the dark lord."

Marie followed the trail of cars as they lurched into the cornfield up ahead. "With this many people, we'll have to fall in line and drive straight through the gates like everyone else. No sneaking over the fence. It'll be easier for you to blend in, though."

Emma pulled her cap down. The line of vehicles crawled by in odd contrast to the farm landscape, and the sound of engines washed out the sway of cornstalks. As the cars approached a large industrial gate, a group of men in dark suits stopped each one short of the entrance. A driver in a green Beetle a few cars up held out a metallic card like the ones they'd found on the dead goons.

Emma looked up at the large smokestack towering over the other side of the gate. Ash and gunk ran down its side like dried lava from a chemical volcano. She pulled the card from her back pocket and set it on her lap. "If we don't make it out of this alive, I just want you to know I appreciate you letting me tag along. And I know this means nothing to you, but I want you to take this." Emma fumbled through her clutch then handed Marie a photo of her brother. "If you find him before I do and have a chance to save him..."

Marie examined the picture. "Cute. As long as he's on the way out, I see no reason not to bring him along, if you go getting yourself murdered." She tucked the picture in her pocket.

Emma laughed to herself. "Thanks. That's reassuring."

As they reached the group of guards, Emma handed her card to Marie and pretended to look out the passenger window, careful to hide her face. Marie rolled down her window and held their ID cards out for the guard. Several agonizing moments later, he handed the cards back.

"Hail, Satan," he said as he waved them through.

"Hail, Satan," Marie replied then jabbed Emma in the ribs.

"Oh, hail, Satan," Emma murmured as Marie rolled up the window.

"You could be a little more convincing," Marie added.

The line of cars trailed into a parking garage on the other side of the second gate, past the dilapidated warehouses and across from the complex. Some derelict buildings had long streaks of rust running down their wavy metal walls. Lit gas torches lined the drive as they approached an austere building up ahead, a beacon in a sea of neglect and obsolescence.

"I've got to find a spot where we won't be blocked in," Marie said. A concrete lot sat to the side of the parking garage, but cars had already filled it to capacity. "Screw it." She pulled out of the line of obedient followers. "What are they going to do—tow me?" She pulled off the concrete and into the dirt next to the full lot, stopping short of a concrete barrier. "Looks like a spot, right?"

"I like your style," Emma replied.

Once Marie cut the engine, she pulled a book from the back seat and opened it to a bookmarked page.

"What's that for?" Emma asked.

"Just making sure I have the words down."

Emma's eyes widened. "What do you mean?"

"This is our diversion."

"Diversion?"

"Yeah. You didn't think I'd just pack a bunch of smoke bombs, did you?"

Emma reached for the door handle but hesitated. "What if someone *does* recognize me?"

"Then I don't have to worry about a distraction." Marie grinned. "Just make a lot of noise."

"Gee, thanks."

Marie looked up from her book. "How many have seen you?"

"I don't know. Just the Reverend and his wife, as far as I know."

Marie was quiet for a moment. "There must be a thousand people here, at least. The odds of someone recognizing you are slim. And if they do, stab them with the pointy end and run." She slipped Emma one of her steel daggers. "Just don't blow my cover."

"Wouldn't dream of it." Emma turned the dagger over in her hand then opened the door and got out of the car.

The imposing concrete structure had been decked out for the occasion. Large black banners hung from the sides of the monolithic warehouse building. Each banner had been emblazoned with a white Leviathan Cross. Black carpet had been rolled down the front steps, and the large metal doors leading inside stood open. They waited in a haphazard line as congregants shuffled inside. Emma shivered with anxiety as the cold wind carried through the crowd. She looked over at Marie, who stood with unflinching confidence.

The luxurious interior of the abandoned warehouse complex contrasted starkly with its rough exterior. The first floor opened to a grand foyer with a crystal chandelier hanging overhead. People gathered in the entryway, chatting in small groups and waiting to enter the main chamber.

"Shit," Emma said under her breath.

"What?" Marie asked.

"Look—the Reverend is standing right there," she whispered. "He'll recognize me."

The Reverend stood at the doors to the sanctuary, shaking hands with his congregants as they entered.

Marie's eyes shifted from side to side. "Looks like those doors are the only way in. Too bad. Guess you'll have to wait in the car."

"I'm not waiting in the freaking car," Emma replied.

"Then march up to him and say hello. I don't know what else you want me to tell you. Just chill out for a minute and look for your opportunity to slip inside. He'll have to go in eventually."

Emma tried to look natural, milling around with the others in the room. She monitored the door, but the

Reverend stood firm, continuing to greet those who entered.

"What a beautiful evening," a woman said to her.

Emma dug deep within and mustered a fake smile. "Yes, it is."

"I told my husband, today will be the first day of the rest of our lives." The woman smiled.

"Hail, Satan." Marie leaned in. "May fire rain down upon the Earth."

"Hail, Satan," the woman replied, reaching out to shake hands. "I'm Carol, nice to meet you. You have to meet my husband." She turned and looked over her shoulder. "Larry!"

Her husband broke free from an awkward circle of middle-aged men shuffling their feet and making small talk in the corner.

"I've just met the two loveliest girls." She turned toward them. "This is Larry, my husband."

"Hail, Satan," Emma said, taking a cue from Marie.

"Hail, Satan," he returned with a half-hearted sigh as his wiry mustache obscured his slight smile.

"Larry's not as into this as I am. I had to *drag* him along with me."

Emma wondered what kind of warped hell she'd wandered into.

"I told you, dear—whatever makes you happy," Larry said.

"I promised him I'd let him buy a motorcycle if he came with me this weekend."

Someone placed a hand on Emma's arm. "If everyone will make their way inside, we're about to begin the service," the woman said.

Thank God.

Emma turned toward the door as the lingering crowd trickled inside. The Reverend must have headed in to prepare for the ceremony, and Emma saw her opportunity to sneak in. Carol's chatter had become whiny background noise as Emma scanned the entrance to ensure that no one familiar stood watching.

"We've got to get inside. Nice to meet you." Emma grabbed Marie by the arm and pulled her toward the door.

"Oh," Carol replied. "Nice to meet you too."

"Such a shame," Marie said as they made their way through the crowd. "I was enjoying our chat."

"You go in first and make sure the Reverend isn't near the door."

When they came to the entryway, Marie peered around the corner then squeezed back through the crowd. "Clear."

Emma stepped over the threshold and into the interior chamber. A long set of stadium-style concrete stairs stretched down toward a central stage. Rows of seats ran along either side of the steps.

The central stage sat against a tall concrete wall

running the width and height of the room. An intricate wooden altar sat along the back wall of the stage. As Emma descended into the chamber, she squinted until she could make out the designs on the altar. The squiggles were actually a sea of writhing snakes carved into the dark-stained wood. At the center, perched on a throne of petrified-looking humans, sat a creature unlike any Emma had ever seen before. The wooden creature's cloven hooves were crossed in front of it and blended into a pair of slender legs. Scales accentuated the toned abs on the creature's torso and cascaded down its body, hanging like the hem of a short skirt. Emma couldn't be sure from the distance, but the figure appeared to have a feminine silhouette, and spiral horns sat atop the creature's head. Four long spears were posted next to the figure, two on either side of it.

I'm going to be sick.

"Would you get going?" Marie pushed her to the next step. "As close to the front as possible."

They continued the descent until they found two empty seats a few rows back from the stage. At the center of the stage sat a round platform shrouded in a black sheet, with another veiled object suspended above it.

"Just keep your head down, and we should be fine," Marie said from behind.

The rest of the crowd acted as if the scene in front of them was ordinary and made small talk as they slowly migrated toward their seats. Organ music poured over the room, and Emma noticed the player perched on a bench in a recessed pit at the front of the stage. The squat woman in a black robe bounced on the piano bench as she hammered the organ keys with passion. Then a hush permeated the crowd as the lights dimmed. Doors at the back slipped shut and smacked against their wooden frames.

Emma took a slow, calming breath as she settled into her seat. Marie showed no signs of fear, as if she'd done this a thousand times before.

The Reverend entered stage right, wearing a black robe embellished with a gilded flame. A slender podium ascended from a trapdoor at the front of the stage, and the Reverend teetered up the steps leading to it. The stage lights shone brightly in his face as he towered over the first few rows of seats. A procession of hooded figures followed, and Emma counted as they stepped across the stage and took seats behind the shrouded platform.

"Where the hell is the book?" Marie whispered.

The Reverend carried nothing more than a small notebook to the podium. "Good evening." His voice boomed through the speakers as he talked into his lapel mic.

The organist cut the music and sat back on her bench.

"Good evening," the crowd echoed in sloppy unison.

Had it not been for the large satanic creature at the front of the stage, Emma would have sworn she was in church back home. The cadence felt so familiar, and she remembered why she'd stopped attending long ago.

"What a special evening it is for us." The Reverend gestured toward the crowd. "When we began construction on this elegant sanctuary, we had no idea that our first ceremony would be our greatest. Hail, Satan!"

"Hail, Satan!" the crowd responded, and Emma mouthed along so as not to draw attention to herself.

"For we have been blessed with a great gift this evening —the ability to call one of our fiery brethren forth to wreak havoc upon those who have given us so much grief in this world. May fire rain down upon them all!" He pounded his fist on the podium.

The congregation broke into sporadic cheers.

"For too long, we have kowtowed to the whims of a Christian nation, a nation that oppresses and condemns those who don't belong and forces us to steep ourselves in temperance, moderation, and humility. Well, that lunacy ends tonight! Hail, Satan!"

"Hail, Satan!" Emma's heart skipped a beat each time the crowd chanted.

"Tonight, the world shall know the name of a new master."

Emma's fingers had gone numb, and her breaths became short and shallow.

"But first, a special announcement for this momentous day." The Reverend beamed. "We have a very special guest in the audience this evening, a guest without whom none of this would have been possible. Let us welcome our uninvited guest to the front of the auditorium, to ensure that she has a proper view of the ceremony."

Emma shot a look at Marie out of the corner of her eye. *Surely they don't mean—*

"Emma." The Reverend held his hand above his brow to block the shade of the spotlight as he looked out into the crowd.

Emma felt as if the air had been sucked from her lungs. She knew it wasn't possible for him to see her through the bright overhead lights, but he somehow seemed to stare right at her. "Surely you didn't think we wouldn't notice."

A glint of metal caught the corner of Emma's eye. Marie had pulled a dagger from under her coat.

Emma looked toward the aisle, but two goons already stood waiting for her.

"I suggest you join us peacefully at the front of the room. If you choose to make things difficult, we will, in turn, make things very difficult for you."

"Just go," Marie whispered as she slid the dagger back into her sleeve and stood to let Emma by.

As Emma reached the edge of the aisle, one of the men yanked her down the steps. The Reverend seemed to have overlooked Marie. He snapped his fingers at several congregants in the first row and waved them away to make room for Emma and her two captors. She felt the outline of the dagger in her coat. They hadn't bothered to search her for weapons.

The Reverend gestured toward the back of the room. "Can we lower the stage lights?" The lights came down as he stepped toward the edge of the stage and leaned over the front row. "So good to see you again. You are in for a treat. If only you'd stayed with us last evening, you could have participated in the ritual. What a shame."

Emma opened her mouth to speak, but no words emerged.

The Reverend turned toward the stage and the cloth-covered forms. "Now, let us prepare the conjuration ritual."

"Hail, Satan," the crowd replied.

He beckoned the shrouded figures to join him at the front of the stage, and together, they pulled the sheet free from the hanging object overhead. A metal cage hung from a ceiling beam, and the person inside shook the iron slats violently.

Emma's heart leapt as she tried to make out the figure. The man had long hair and definitely wasn't Adam. His feet hung loose through the gaps in the cage. "I'll kill you!" he shouted at the figures below, an empty threat considering his circumstances.

The Reverend looked up at the cage. "You have no idea how special you are, my boy. Your blood will set us all free!"

"You're a psychopath! Let me out of here." The expression on his panic-stricken face was clear from the first row as he looked out at the large audience.

"You will be free soon enough," the Reverend continued.

The man spit through the bottom of the cage and caught the Reverend in the forehead. The attendants moved in and ushered him away from the cage.

"It's fine." The Reverend wiped his face with the sleeve of his robe. He turned toward the crowd. "The dangers of unwilling sacrifices." He chuckled as he stepped back toward the cage, careful not to stand directly underneath. "Please prepare the ceremonial pikes."

The hooded figures positioned themselves on either side of the altar of the wooden creature, and each pulled a pike free from its mount. They stood under the metal cage as the man above continued to struggle.

"Please, remove the ceremonial cloth," the Reverend said.

The attendants moved in and pulled the sheet loose from the circular platform.

"Although most conjurings only require one sacrifice, tonight's very special event requires two participants to complete the ceremony. I'd planned for our unexpected guest to serve as a second, but she was unavailable, unfortunately."

Oohs and aahs came from the crowd as the shroud fell in a heap onto the floor. Feet hung over the edge of the platform, but the angle made it impossible to see the figure tied atop it. The Reverend hit a foot pedal on the ground, and gears ground at its base, clinking like a roller coaster slowly climbing the tracks. The platform lurched, lifted into the air, and tilted forward just enough for Emma to see Adam's face.

_____

CHAPTER FIFTEEN

Emma clenched a cry between her teeth. Adam's face had been beaten and bruised, and one of his eyes had swollen shut. She tried to rise from her chair, but one of the guards held her firm.

Adam's legs were bound and his arms stretched to the side, forming a crude crucifix. He wore the same white linen as the man in the cage, and his hands had been forced into fists, each gripping a bright white candle. A metal cap kept his head close to the table. It reminded Emma of the ones they'd used in electric-chair executions. Unlike the man in the cage, Adam didn't protest, but Emma could just make out the rapid rise and fall of his chest. He was alive at least.

"And now for the book." The Reverend grinned widely. "Let's welcome tonight's acolytes. They've been practicing hard all day for this."

The coos coming from the crowd made Emma sick to her stomach. Two children emerged from the stage door, propelled by a set of adult hands. A child with blond hair peeking out from under the hood of his black robe gripped a long brass staff with bell-shaped metal affixed to the top and a lit wick protruding from its curve. He stepped forward and stretched to light the candles in each of Adam's hands.

The second acolyte gripped a purple satin bag and held it up to the Reverend, who reached in and retrieved the leather book with the human face. Adam seemed to come to and fought against his restraints. He craned his neck, but the cap held him firmly to the platform.

The Reverend motioned for the children to return to the stage door and stepped back to the podium. He lifted the book high in the air. "Behold, our key to eternal bliss. Those who've mocked us will look back on this day with terror."

Cheers came from the crowd with scattered calls of "Hail, Satan."

"This book shall—"

A shrill ringing filled the room as the lights died, leaving the audience in complete darkness. Emma put her hands to her ears and fell to the floor, but the sound seemed to be coming from inside her own head. The lights flashed, and Emma looked up toward the stage. The Reverend clung to the side of the podium, his knuckles white from his intense grip. Marie knelt next to him, grimoire in hand.

"Help!" he pled into the microphone. As he fell backward down the podium stairs, he grabbed at the dagger that pinned his black robe to his side.

Desperate screams filled the air as the crowd panicked, and Emma reached for the dagger underneath her coat. One of Emma's guards had already scrambled toward the stage, and the other crept toward her as he regained his footing. Emma didn't have time to think. As the guard lunged for her, she pulled the dagger free and held it out to defend herself. The blade caught him just under the chin, and a spurt of blood splashed her face. Emma let out a terrified scream as the man frantically pawed at the handle sticking out of his neck. As he fell limp next to her, Emma grabbed the dagger handle, closed her eyes, and pulled.

The second guard climbed the stage steps as Marie turned toward the attendants. The hooded figures fumbled with their pikes, but the long ceremonial weapons were no match for Marie's agility. Marie pulled a dagger from her boot and wove between the four of them, knocking their pointed weapons aside as they flailed in her direction. She hit the first executioner in the chest then twisted round and hit the second in the stomach.

Emma's blood-covered hands shook as she recovered her footing and chased after the second guard. She lunged, propelled by pure adrenaline, and hooked the dagger into the guard's back. This time wasn't so easy, though. The guard swung around wildly and caught Emma in the side of the head with his elbow. She tumbled down the stairs and hit the concrete floor hard as the guard ripped the dagger from his back then threw it aside.

On stage, the two remaining executioners rounded the ceremonial platform. Marie leapt atop it, jumping over Adam and onto one of the figures, whom she tagged in the chest. The final executioner, seeing his numbers quickly dwindling, dropped the pike and leapt off the side of the stage then shuffled into the chaotic crowd making its way to the back exit.

Emma backed against the first row of seats, but the guard was on top of her before she could regain her footing. As he pinned her against the chair, she frantically clawed at his face, catching him hard across his left eye. He reared back and grunted, but when he leaned in to attack once more, Marie pulled his hair from behind and swiped the dagger across his throat.

Emma squirreled free from under him and recovered her weapon on the way to the stage. The side of her head throbbed as she reached Adam's platform. She pulled a candle loose from his hand and tossed it to the ground with a splatter of white wax. "I'm getting you out of here." She wasn't sure she could deliver on the promise.

Although his left eye had been swollen shut, a sliver of

his bright-blue iris shone through his right. "Save yourself," he whispered.

"There's no way I'm leaving you behind." She pulled the straps free from his arm.

As soon as his arm fell free, he reached for Emma's. "You don't understand. It's already done. They made me drink it." He coughed. "They've said his name. I can feel it inside. It's growing." A tear trickled down his puffed cheek.

Emma pulled back in horror. "What are you talking about?"

He placed his palm on her cheek. "It's feeding on me. You have to leave me and get out of here."

Emma leaned in to loosen the strap around his waist. "I can't leave you behind."

Several men in black suits fought against the exodus, working their way closer to the stage.

"You have to go before it's too late," he grunted. "You don't have much—"

A cry came from the side of the stage as Marie fell backward through the doorway and onto her back. Yvonne emerged, brandishing a bloody knife.

Emma felt a sharp pain in her thigh, and her leg buckled underneath her.

"You will not ruin this!" the Reverend shouted as he dropped the bloody pike to the floor and crawled toward her, his gown glistening with a growing patch of crimson.

Emma tried to stand, but the Reverend caught her by

the hair and pulled so hard she felt the sting of roots tearing free. He yanked her toward him and twisted himself around as he climbed on top of her and wrapped his hand around her throat.

She tried to free herself from the Reverend's grip, but he held firm, and even though she landed a few firm blows to the side of his face, his resolve was unwavering. Darkness emerged at the corners of Emma's eyes as the combination of panic and lack of oxygen began to work its terrible magic. Yvonne stood in the background, gripping a ceremonial pike and thrusting it rabidly into the suspended cage.

Emma looked down at the Reverend's torso, where the dagger still hung from the side of his gut. With her last bit of strength, she reached for the dagger and twisted it deeper into the Reverend's stomach. He screamed and reared back on his haunches, and Emma ripped the dagger free from his body. The Reverend's eyes went bloodshot, and with a primal cry, he attacked once more, and Emma met him with the dagger.

The man in the cage overhead, once animated and thrashing, now lay still as the life force ran out of him and dripped down onto Adam below. As the blood spattered onto the platform, it filled a deep circular groove surrounding Adam's body.

Yvonne dropped the pike and turned toward Emma.

"It's done," she said through gritted teeth. Her eyes

flashed to the Reverend, and her expression went slack. "I'll kill you, you little bitch!" She rushed toward Emma, brandishing the knife she'd used on Marie.

Emma searched frantically for another weapon, but her dagger lay buried underneath the Reverend. As Yvonne barreled toward her, Emma dropped to the floor and lifted the ceremonial pike lying next her. The weapon caught Yvonne in the chest. Yvonne dropped the book and her dagger, and Emma thrust the pike deeper into her and pushed her off the stage onto the concrete floor.

The Reverend's goons closed in as Emma reached for the book and turned toward the altar. The circle of blood around Adam's body had caught fire, spewing ruby-red flame into the atmosphere. Light shone through his chest as if someone were shining a flashlight from inside him. His screams echoed off the walls of the cavernous room as his skin sizzled around his belly button until the burn covered his entire body.

Emma frantically flipped through the book, but it was impossible to tell which of the hundreds of pages was the correct one.

Flame burst from Adam's chest and spiraled outward, consuming his body and sending a fiery tornado toward the ceiling. Tentacles shot from the fiery portal, slapping down toward Emma and knocking the book loose from her hands.

Tears obscured Emma's vision. She fumbled for the

book as an undulating beast pulled free from Adam's body and crashed down onto the stage.

"It's beautiful," a man said, his voice barely audible over the sound of crunching wood and hissing flame.

The Reverend's goons stood at the edge of the stage, blocking Emma's path to the back of the auditorium and admiring the scene unfolding in front of them. A crowd approached, holding their hands up to the mammoth beast. The creature shrieked—from where, Emma couldn't tell— and brought a tentacle down on top of them, crushing some and sending others airborne. The ground shook behind her as the creature struck once more, sending shards of plastic seating flying.

"We've got to go!" Marie braced herself against the wall next to the side door and held a hand tightly to her bloody side. "We need more time!"

Emma wiped the mixture of smoke and tears from her eyes and focused on the stage door. Then she lunged across the stage toward Marie, and the creature swung down hard, rattling the floor under her feet and narrowly missing her.

The side door opened to a staging room, where several robes hung in an open wardrobe and books lined a ceremonial table. She bolted toward the door on the far side, which led to a narrow hallway ending in a set of steps going up. Emma's heart fluttered as she helped Marie down the beige hallway toward their only chance at freedom. "Are you okay?"

"Just a little bloody. I'll be fine," Marie panted.

They climbed the stairs and burst through the metal door at the top. Cold night air hit Emma's face as people scrambled to their cars outside, causing a line of traffic that extended past the vacant buildings and out through the front exit. She spotted their car in the distance as the screams and sounds of twisting metal carried up the staircase.

Her thigh throbbed as she limped toward their car underneath the full blood moon that hung two sizes too large in the sky. The front of the complex exploded in a blast of glass, concrete, and sharp metal shards, and a shriek echoed through the air as the creature emerged from the debris.

Emma passed the line of cars waiting for escape, and as she reached her vehicle, she heard the creature tearing through the congregants behind her. Had it not been for the imminent danger, Emma would have found satisfaction in seeing the creature rip through its own followers.

Marie tossed her the keys. "Give me the book. You drive."

By the time Emma climbed into the driver's seat, the pain in her thigh had become unbearable. She stopped to catch her breath. She looked at the complex through her windshield and listened to the shrieks as they once again came closer.

"Is it chasing us?" She immediately received her answer as the ground shook behind her. "It knows we have the book." She twisted the key in the ignition, and the engine turned over. Emma looked hopelessly at the line in front of her. The creature would catch up before she could reach the gate. "Hold on. We're going through the fence."

"Just do it." Marie groaned next to her as she tried to staunch the flow of blood.

Emma shifted the car into drive, ignoring the line of cars trying to make their way out through the main gate, and aimed the black vehicle at the chain-link fence. Her car's tires whirred on the dirt as she pressed the pedal to the floor with the creature closing in behind her. She sped over the dirt mound to avoid other cars, and her bumper bottomed out on the other side. When her hood struck the flimsy metal gate, the support posts ripped free, and the car slid under the chain link like an eager dog tunneling toward freedom.

A small clearing preceded the cornstalks, and Emma braced herself as she drove straight toward them. The stalks buckled under the car's bumper, snapping and dragging against its undercarriage as Marie flipped through the book to the appropriate page. The leaves of the stalks slapping against the side of the car created a hissing noise that reminded Emma of the cicadas that came every decade or so.

The car slowed and stuttered under the constant barrage of corn stalks. As Emma reached the edge of the field, she looked into the rearview mirror. Behind them, the beast flung escaping cars aside as it flattened the cornstalks bordering the road.

When Emma reached the main road, cars lined both lanes as people tried to make their escape. She didn't hesitate, couldn't hesitate, and took the embankment up to the road head-on, aiming for the small gap between two crawling vehicles. The seat belt snapped taut as the car bottomed out after clearing the gap.

They'd come barreling out of the cornfield about a quarter mile from the curvy road to the house on the hill. Adrenaline surged through Emma, numbing the pain in her thigh and collarbone.

Marie's face had gone pale, and beads of sweat ran down her forehead. "If we can make it to the house, its protections might slow the thing down long enough for us to read the passage." She ran her hand along her side and stared down at her bloody palm.

Screams and crunching metal permeated the landscape as Emma reached the road to Rosalie's. The creature slammed against the trees behind them. The sturdy trunks were no match for the pulsating tentacles that ripped their roots from the ground and cast them aside like plastic toys, but they seemed to slow the beast.

As the wrought-iron gates came into view, Emma's spirit lifted. The gates creaked open as if the woman of the house had been waiting for them and slammed shut as soon as they'd driven through to the front yard. When the creature crossed into the clearing on the opposite side of the gate, Emma slipped out of the car and got her first real look. The thing slithered across the ground with a set of thrashing tentacles that grew out of a sagging humanlike torso. It tossed a tree aside with one of its two clawed arms. An elongated skull with sunken eyes sat atop the beast's slumped shoulders. A slack-jawed mouth hung loose and swayed from side to side as if it had been broken. A sharp front tooth extended from the thing's lips like a beak. The creature itself seemed to have grown bigger since it had crawled free from Adam's body, and it towered over the front gate at nearly twice its original height.

"I can't do it." Marie laid the open book on the driver's seat. "You have to read it. Face the thing, and read the entire passage."

Emma grabbed the book and squinted in the moon-light. When the creature butted against the gate, it jolted backward as if the gate had been electrified. Emma's body cast a shadow against the bright headlight beams as she looked down at the winding passage—written in Latin, she thought—and started to read aloud. But the creature persisted, making the gate buckle as it struck repeatedly with its heavy tentacles.

Help me was Emma's telepathic plea, for nothing else stood between her and the demon threatening to destroy her. She concentrated on the passage in front of her, reading as quickly as she could as the creature broke through and slunk along the front yard, its tentacles sticking to the blessed earth that seared its skin upon contact. The smell of putrid roasting meat filled the night air as the beast ripped itself free from the ground, leaving bits of flesh behind and continuing the slow slog toward Emma.

But with the smell came something else—the scent of burning sage followed by a trail of smoke wafting from the backyard. As smoke billowed around the house, the creature slowed as if repulsed by it, its tentacles sizzling as they lingered on the gravel path.

Emma choked on the smell of a thousand bundles of sage burning all at once but kept reading. Her words filled her own ears as if the cosmos was whispering them back to her, and as the creature edged toward her and raised a tentacle to strike, she completed the page.

Although she knew the act would be futile, Emma tried to shield her face as a tentacle came down. But the beast's writhing appendage snapped back as if hitting an invisible wall. The creature tried to strike again as Emma braced herself for impact, but the hit bounced once more, sending the beast slithering backward.

The ground rumbled under Emma's feet as the creature backed into the yard. Wind whipped through the trees, and the shutters rattled against the house's aging walls. Emma's ears popped as she stepped out into the yard and lifted her head to the sky—a sky that pulled toward the creature like a piece of fabric snagged at the center.

The sage smoke spiraled around the stellar stalactite, and the thing's arms lifted upward toward it. The beast tried to pull away, but the force was too strong, and when the two touched, the sky opened into a black void above the creature's head. The thing let out a shriek, and its sizzling skin clung to the ground as it tried to anchor itself.

But as the portal consumed the beast's head, the creature lost its grip and was pulled free, bringing bits of earth with it as if the portal were a cosmic vacuum cleaner. Once the last tentacle had slipped through, the portal closed, and the sloping sky shot upward toward the heavens, back to its proper place, trailed by wisps of lingering sage smoke.

Emma stepped farther away from the house and into the spot in the yard where the creature had once stood, the smoke making her eyes water. Grass had been ripped from the yard, leaving large divots where the creature had dug itself in. She moved to the car and examined the damage to the front end then crouched in the driver's-side door.

"This thing probably won't make it very far. We should —" She looked at Marie, who lay slumped against the passenger door, her eyes gray and vacant. "Marie," Emma said as if saying her name would bring her back, but the woman simply stared ahead with her hands slack in her lap. Emma's eyes were drawn to a tangle of keys in the driver's seat. Marie must have left them for her to find. As she slowly backed away from the car, the dead woman's eyes seemed to follow her as the evening chill penetrated her body.

She turned toward the house, which seemed to look back at her with the same solemn expression as smoke swirled around its edges. She sensed Rosalie watching her, grieving with her. She fell to her knees as hot tears streamed, and her scream echoed off the house and through the clearing as images of death and destruction flashed before her eyes.

Then she pulled herself to her feet and opened the front door. She passed through the foyer, the smell of sage wafting through the house. The sage garden sat in crispy ruin, the earth scorched where fire had ripped through, and some plants were still burning in Emma's peripheral vision.

She climbed the stairs to her bedroom, her body aching with every step. Although she had cleaned her room several times, a decade's worth of dust still clung in places, and a cloud puffed outward as she slid her duffel bag from under the bed. She pulled her clothes from the dresser and shoved her remaining belongings into it, including the shitty laptop that had failed to function since shortly after her arrival.

As she reached the hallway, she hesitated then turned toward the staircase to the third floor and climbed to Rosalie's bedroom. She stood in the doorway and spoke into the black. "I'm sorry we've caused so much trouble. I promise I'll make sure the book makes it to the right people." Her stomach lurched. "And if you see my brother, tell him I love him but that he's still an asshole." She wiped the corners of her eyes.

She descended the staircase, and a gust of wind passed through the hall as if the house was letting out a deep sigh. The floorboards underneath her groaned as she walked to the foyer, gathered Marie's belongings, and shoved them into her leather bag.

Emma walked outside and headed to Marie's yellow convertible, which still sat perched in the front yard. She sorted through the keys to find the right one and unlocked the door. Then she set the book in the passenger seat. Its pages were covered with Marie's blood.

Emma looked up at the house one last time through the windshield. It seemed to sag even more than it had before that night. *It must be tired,* she thought. Centuries of protecting the book had taken a toll on the structure and the family who'd once lived inside. She saw Rosalie once again, standing behind the third-floor window, looking longingly into the front yard.

Emma slid the key into the ignition and turned it. The convertible roared to life.

Light flickered behind Rosalie, and the room grew brighter. It wasn't heavenly salvation coming to take her to the promised land but rather a fire slowly working its way up the woman's frame until it consumed the window entirely. Once the fire had finished with Rosalie, it spread rapidly throughout the home as if fueled by a spectral accelerant.

As Emma turned the car around, flames broke through the roof tiles and lapped upward toward the heavens, sending a plume of black smoke and embers into the night sky. She rolled the windows down to listen for any signs of the Reverend's congregation, but the night was eerily quiet, and the wind carried through the trees as it had on her first night at the house.

She reached the main road. A path of scorched destruction extended into the distance as overturned cars speckled the cornfield. She passed a group of petrified church members as a police car, ambulance, and fire truck were setting up at the scene. A police officer waved Emma through, past a set of road flares.

She rolled down her window. "What happened, officer?"

"To be honest, I'm not sure, ma'am. We think maybe a gas explosion."

"Check that warehouse down the road. Rumor is, these people have been up to some dark stuff out that way. Good luck, sir." Not waiting for him to respond, she accelerated toward the highway.

Emma drove for a solid hour before stopping at a gas station to use her brother's cellphone. Although she'd driven far enough to have escaped the Reverend's reach, she still scanned the area around her to ensure that no one had followed.

She tapped an entry in her brother's contact list.

"Hello." The voice was female this time. It didn't have the same exhausted timbre as the man's, perhaps signifying she was more capable of her job.

"I have the book," Emma replied.

"Marie?" the woman asked.

"She's gone. Killed, I mean, but I wouldn't have made it without her. None of this would have been possible without her. My brother too." Her voice cracked. After a long pause, Emma spoke once more. "Hello?"

"I'm sorry," the woman replied. "I—"

"Look, I just need to know where to take this thing."

"Are you at the house? We can have someone there—"

"The house is burning to the ground. I'm on the road. I'll bring it to you."

"Of course." The woman's voice wavered. "Can you

take down an address?"

Emma pulled a pen from her bag. "Go ahead."

The woman rattled off an address in Massachusetts, and Emma wrote it down. "That'll take me a while, maybe a day or two of driving."

"That's fine. If you run into trouble, you have our number."

That's reassuring. "Thanks," Emma said half-heartedly.

"Marie should have had a special key with her. Did you find an odd-looking key?"

"Maybe on her key ring." Emma flipped through the keys hanging from the ignition. The car key sat next to a few standard ones, and after that was a skeleton key. "With a spiral handle?"

"You'll need it to drop the book. We'll take it from there. The key will get you into the building. Is there anything else I can do to help?"

Emma paused. "Yeah, bring my brother back," she replied, pulling the receiver away. But before she hung up, she put it to her face once more. "And I'm still expecting the rest of the ten grand and a few more for my trouble. It's the least you could do."

"We are truly deeply—"

Emma ended the call. Before leaving the station, she purchased the largest energy drink she could find. *It's going to be a long night.*

CHAPTER SIXTEEN

The book sat on the passenger seat like a ticking bomb as the sun broke over the horizon. Emma sped down the highway toward her final destination somewhere in the western tip of Massachusetts. She'd driven through the night, making only a few stops for the restroom and coffee.

Emma's thoughts closed in on her—thoughts of her brother ripped apart by a celestial being, thoughts of breaking the news to her parents, and thoughts of the end of the world and how close she'd been to it. And by the time the sun hung highest in the sky, those thoughts became too much to bear. She flipped the switch on the radio and twisted the dial as stations faded in and out until the sad strumming of an electric guitar took her breath away. The dulcet tones of Jeff Buckley singing "Hallelujah" drifted through her speakers and into her eardrums.

She'd forced her brother to listen to that song a hundred times before.

"You know I'm an atheist," he said.

"You're missing the point. It's not religious at all," she'd shot back. "The song's about love and loss and pushing through the pain—finding light at the end of the tunnel."

"Still sounds Jesusy to me."

A car honked as Emma lurched into the lane next to her. Her vision blurred, and she wiped tears from her eyes with one hand and jerked the car back into the proper lane with the other.

By the time Emma pulled through town, afternoon had slipped into early evening, and her fifth cup of coffee had gone cold. Her stomach cramped from the onslaught of acid and lack of food. She needed a doctor, and the gash in her thigh had garnered an odd look from a gas station attendant when she stopped to purchase bandages and rubbing alcohol.

She scanned the street for addresses as the GPS on Adam's phone guided her toward the mysterious destination. The busy street stretched into the center of the city, with historic brick buildings crammed next to each other. She could have spotted the building without a GPS. A stained-glass eye sat in the center of the cathedral-like window of the brick structure. Although the building had some characteristics of a church, it lacked a steeple, and crosshatched patterns protruded from walls that stretched farther than any of the other buildings on the block. Had Emma been a passerby, she would have assumed the place was a church, but her gut said otherwise.

She pulled the car into a parallel spot and grabbed the book from the passenger seat, ignoring the meter completely as she parked. She walked up to the stone steps leading to the front door.

Locked. She fished out the odd skeleton key and slipped it inside the lock. The latch clicked, and she gripped the metal handle and pushed. The creak of the door hinges echoed through the cavernous space on the other side.

The interior looked as if it hadn't been updated since the place's construction. Tall wooden bookshelves, stuffed to capacity, lined the walls and ran up toward the vaulted ceiling. She saw her reflection in the polished marble floor that stretched to an altar at the far end of the building. Reading tables speckled the room. She received an odd stare from a man poring over a table of open books.

Emma stepped cautiously toward the altar at the back of the room as if a wrong move would cause the floor to drop out from under her or trigger a rolling boulder. When she had reached the midway point, another man emerged from a side door and scurried toward her.

"Excuse me." His eyes scanned her blood-caked clothing. "Can I help you?"

Emma swallowed hard. "Just came to make a deposit." She held the leather face of the book up for him to see.

His expression soured as his eyes darted from the book to Emma then back again.

"You've come alone?"

"Alone," she replied.

The man's eyes went glossy as he stepped aside. "Very well, then." He gestured toward the altar ahead.

Emma followed the narrow path between the tables until she reached the wooden altar—only it wasn't like any altar she'd seen before. A column stretched up from the floor and had been carved with intricate lines and dashes. The top of the altar was, in fact, an empty tray, and she spotted a hole for the key just below it.

Emma set the book inside the tray and ran her fingers over the bloodstained cover. She slid the key inside the keyhole and twisted. Then the floor began to tremble underneath her as the sound of clinking gears came from below. In one swift motion, the tray was sucked down into the altar and disappeared into a long track-lined chute. A few minutes later, the tray returned, empty and ready for the next deposit.

Emma turned toward the aisle and began the slow march to the front door. The man waited for her and held his hand out as she approached.

She pulled the intricate key loose from the key ring and

dropped it into his hand. "I need the car. It's my only way home."

The man nodded as his fingers closed around the key.

"She wouldn't have admitted this, but she saved me," Emma said, "and if it wasn't for her—if she hadn't shown me how to stop it—I'd be dead, and that thing would still be loose."

"She was one of our best." He looked down at her bloodstained pants. "You ought to have someone look at that. We have people who can—"

Emma held up her hand to silence him. "I just need to get home. I'll deal with it later."

"Take care of yourself," he said as she reached for the door.

Once she was outside, the cool evening air felt like freedom. Emma sucked it in until it filled her lungs as she returned to the convertible. She revved the engine, pulled a U-turn, and headed toward the highway. As the car sped up, she patted the seat next to her.

He would have loved this car.

Memories of road trips with Adam flashed through her mind. A trip to the Grand Canyon with their family had resulted in hours of pestering each other. Her older brother had been too cool and too mature to play with her. Things changed when he got his license and their parents gifted him their old compact.

"Want to go for a ride?" he asked, jingling the keys in front of her.

"You're kidding, right?" she'd asked. He was always kidding.

"Not kidding. I thought we could get some ice cream and stop by the park or something."

What she would have given for one more joy ride.

CHAPTER SEVENTEEN

Emma stood on the soft grass in the dreary New York morning, her flats sinking slightly into the damp earth. The patch of disturbed dirt in front of her still hadn't settled, and large chunks of mud and clay protruded from the ground like miniature mountains. It would take another few weeks at least for the cemetery to put the headstone in, and for the moment, her brother's death seemed temporary.

Grief settled in like an unwelcome relative, promising to stay for only a few days but lingering for what seemed like an eternity. She knelt and placed a rose across the dirt patch and stood back. Her parents must have come again this week, since toy cars had been laid out in a neat square pattern around the uneven dirt. Breaking the news to them had been the second-worst moment of her life, the first being the satanic ceremony itself, the memories of which bubbled up in every nightmare.

Whenever she went to the graveyard with her parents, her mom spoke to Adam as if he were listening. And after all the time Emma had spent at the house in the woods—time filled with spirits and demons—she wondered if perhaps he was. That small nugget of hope was sometimes just enough to drive her forward.

Rain drizzled as she walked to the yellow convertible. For all Emma knew, the Aurora still sat in front of the charred house in the woods—two relics of previous lives. Emma still wondered what secret society lurked in the shadows and how many more houses were perched on mysterious hilltops in faraway countrysides, each of them containing books with immeasurable power. Sometimes she wished she could forget it all and go back to a time when her biggest concerns were writing her book and making the rent payment.

EMMA MARVELED as the clerk carefully stacked books in the window display at the Book Cellar. *The Haunting at Sage House*. She still hated the title, but her publisher said it would sell.

"You need the word *house* in the title, and we have to have a creepy house on the cover. People will eat it up."

The book had been marketed as fiction. "It's the only way it'll sell," her agent told her, and Emma had little clout with which to protest.

Although the book hadn't brought in the dough needed to quit her retail job, it did provide enough of a cushion for her to continue to write part-time without the fear of starving or missing rent. She sipped her cup of hazelnut coffee and reveled in the moment before stepping through the front door and down to the main level. A table waited for her at the back of the store, stacked with books—her books with her name and her story.

She loved the smell of bookstores, although nothing would ever compare to the smell of the library at Sage House and the scent of hundreds of years of history wafting through the air in swirling whiffs of aged leather and yellowed paper. Only five or six people stood in line, but to Emma, it might as well have been a hundred. She waved to eager fans, most of whom had brought their own books with them. Some of their copies were even dog-eared and worn as if they'd been read several times.

When she sat at the table and gestured for the atten-dant to let the first person approach, she glanced up through the windows of the store. Her brother stood peering through the glass from the other side. Emma held his gaze.

A woman approached the man and tugged at his arm. He turned toward her and pecked her on the cheek then stepped away from the window and continued his journey down the shopping street.

Since Adam's death, she'd seen him in nearly every slim twentysomething male with jet-black hair—at the coffee shop, at the gas station, and in her dreams.

Emma turned to the eager woman standing in front of her. "Sorry."

"I loved your book." The words came in such a flurry that Emma had a hard time telling them apart.

"Thank you so much. It's nice to meet you." She pulled the cap off her marker. "To whom should I make this out?"

After the signing, Emma sat at the table and traced the title on a hardback copy of her book. The day should have been everything she had ever dreamed of, but the pomp and circumstance felt oddly hollow. Although she wished to forget the events at Sage House, life would never be simple again. Aside from the loss of her brother, she'd been cursed with the knowledge that a sinister world lay just beyond the shadows. And even though she had accomplished a dream, that dream no longer seemed to hold the same meaning.

As Emma pushed through the doors of the bookstore and crossed the street to her car, she noticed a figure leaning against it. For a moment, she swore the woman wearing the vest and crimson pants was Marie. She blinked hard to try to erase the hallucination, but the woman remained.

"Can I help you?"

"I read your book," the woman replied. "You got a few details wrong."

"Look, if you're mad about the book, then—"

"We're not mad. And if I'm not mistaken, your book is in the fiction section. If you hadn't published the book, we never would have found you." She slapped the hood of the convertible. "Although you might have considered changing vehicles."

Emma clenched her fists. "What do you want?"

"I think a better question would be, what do you want?"

Emma cocked her head.

"We've had outsiders tangled up in reclamations before. Those lucky enough to survive usually skip town or fall off the face of the Earth. You could have moved on with your life, but you chose to surround yourself with what happened in Rudder."

"What's your point?"

"My point is that you got a taste for what it's like to save the world, and you can't let it go. You're still driving around in Marie's car."

"Look, I don't have time for—"

The woman held up her hand. "Join us. If we've learned anything from Sage House, it's that we have to move faster to consolidate the remaining texts. If you really want to honor your brother, you'll put your little stories aside and make sure no one has to experience what he went through—what his family went through."

Emma stepped back. "I don't understand. Why me?"

"Somehow, you managed to face a tier-one demon and walk away with little more than a few scratches. We need you. We can train you." The woman held out an odd-looking skeleton key with a spiral handle. "It's yours if you want it."

Emma stared at the key but refused to move.

The woman approached until she and Emma were face-to-face. "Look me in the eye and tell me that you're happy with your life, that you don't feel a sinking feeling in your gut first thing every morning and last thing at night. You've seen the truth and know deep down that no matter how hard you try to ignore it, the darkness is coming for you—for all of us. You can do something about it, or you can wait for it to come knocking."

Emma swiped the key from the woman's hand.

The woman's lips curled into a smile. "Let's get going, then. We've got lots of work to do."

ENJOY THE BOOK?

Check Out Chris Cooper's Other Books

Nobody's Ghost

The Dreadful Objects

The Oliver Crum Trilogy

Please Consider Leaving a Review

Reviews help tremendously. Please consider leaving a review on Amazon or Goodreads!

Want to Stay in Touch?

Visit Dreadfulmedia.com to join our mailing list, report errors, or just say hello.

ABOUT THE AUTHOR

Chris Cooper is a writer, college professor, novice coffee roaster, and recovering engineer. He lived and worked in Japan, where he developed an obscure obsession for fancy fountain pens and currently lives in Ohio with his partner and Australian Cattle Terrier. Both enjoy going for walks. Chris writes horror and supernatural thrillers full of colorful three-dimensional characters, macabre adventures, and twisty turny plots.